A TIGER'S TAIL

The Trigger

Alexis POE

ISBN: 9798665271552

Cover design by: Art Painter
Library of Congress Control Number: 2018675309
Printed in the United States of America

I

In the grand scheme of things, I would declare that the events that kick-started this idea of keeping memoirs of some delectable encounters I have had over the years were purely accidental. However, I would also admit that some of these encounters left indelible impacts on me while some have been quite impersonal, albeit sometimes therapeutic to some of my clients. Others; you might say were neither. This is just my opinion. You draw your own conclusions and whatever wisdom you might be able to glean from any of them.

This coincidental first event was not intended by any means. I will explain....

One bright Tuesday afternoon, I had just cleared my desk and my schedule for five days. I decided to give myself a good well-deserved holiday. I went to this discrete and discreet luxury pad for a quiet self-indulgent one. Notice my play on words there?

Where is it, you might ask?

But if I told you, it wouldn't be discreet then, would it?

I had just checked into my hotel room around 1:30pm and decided to sit by the bar and loll the time away when I saw him come into the lobby. He had two people with him – a man and a woman. They chatted briefly with him. He shook hands with the man. The woman nodded to him. It was obvious she didn't want to shake hands. The couple then strolled away. He strolled quietly towards the bar. I couldn't help noticing slight signs of wear around the edges – faint signs that could be missed if you didn't know him. But I knew him ... well ... sort of. I will clarify ...

I had met David Reynolds three times in my life. The first time was in a party organized by this up and coming society girl who enjoyed the company of the posh boys; Becky – I think – her name was. She always threw these parties at least once every three months. It was the weekend highlight in town. Everybody who was anybody wanted to be there. She owned her own boutique on the high street so I presumed she could afford it. I don't know and I didn't care. It was always in this upscale night club in Soho. It became such a hit, she had to hire party bouncers to control overflow. It was strictly on invitation. I couldn't believe it when I got one. Don't ask me how it happened.

He created such a buzz when he waltzed in with his ilk that I turned from chatting with a mate in curiosity. He had this gentle confident disposition about him. I remember saying in my mind that night 'Wow! Who is this Mr debonair?'

An air of niceness, yet naughty swirled around him as much as the friends that tagged along everywhere he went. I knew at once I would want to get to know this guy. And I wasn't the only one. All the young girls in the room seemed to convey the same by the way they smiled when he glided smoothly past them.

"Who's that?" I had asked my date Jairus, some guy I met through an acquaintance.

He unenthusiastically told me.

"He must be famous" I added, fishing for information without making it obvious

"He is supposed to be the *life* of the party" Jairus said doing the inverted commas with his fingers "He and those stupid four friends of his; 'Chelsea' boys living off their parents fortunes. They think they are the centre of the universe the way they carry on"

Didn't look like that from where I was standing. The respect in his eyes when he smiled at someone did not look like someone who looked down his nose at people. Looked more like Jairus was envious. Well ... he needed to be. I was strongly attracted to this guy. So strongly I smiled in resonance when he smiled at some girl in the crowd. He pecked her on the brow. I involuntarily scratched my brow.

"What does he do?" I asked

"I hear he's into a lot of things. Like I said, his father's fortunes"

Jairus mumbled

Well, some children squander their father's money, so credit to him, I thought.

He swept past me with a slight nod and a smile, shook my mate's hand, chatted briefly and mixed with the crowd. Don't get me wrong. I was one of the most beautiful girls at the party but I guess he was respecting the fact I was with someone. Good character trait I'd say. That did not deter me, nonetheless. I was intent on getting to know him before the night was over …

Needless to say, I got drunk sometime later, made a total fool of myself and was kicked out of the party. My reputation in the circles was destroyed and I never got to meet him again …

Until now.

Three years had passed. I was now a registered Psychiatrist in private practice with a part time advice column in one of the newspapers. I was doing well. But I never forgot David. I never met another man quite like him; probably because of the kind look he gave me even as I was being thrown out that night for messing up. Men usually don't do that; especially men like him with the money and fancy clothes. They will tread you underfoot and not bother to clean their shoes. I know because I have met quite a few … nothing to discuss.

As I sat there pondering about the past, he nonchalantly strolled over to the bar, sat down and ordered a drink. I pretended not to notice in case he was interested in picking me up. Don't get me wrong, but what else would anyone be doing in a hotel like this? Alone? …

Yes; that's why I was here. I am a single, hard-working lady who had not had a reasonable holiday in three years. I also had not had a relationship in the same amount of time. Not even a fling. You may say that's pathetic. I'd prefer to say I've been very busy building my career to bother with little things like that. But once in a while, your body tends to crave for a little skirmish. In my case, more than 'once in a while'. I'm not going to explain that any further. Unfortunately, men tend to be overwhelmed by the authority air around me; the respect and power I command; the intelligence I display and ….

6

Okay; Maybe I am sounding off a bit, aren't I?

Let's just say … my chastity belt was killing me now and I needed a bit of … you know… unwinding? Let's just say that. And who else to mingle with but your crush of shady past?

He never glanced my way.

"Hi" I tried. "Don't I know you from somewhere?"

He sighed and dropped his shoulders: a gesture I understood too well. It meant either "now what?" or "not again" or "… for goodness sakes…". Being who he is, I can understand the irritability of always being the centre of the stage. It's like Tom Cruise being recognized in a party gathering. Not as exciting to him as you might think. I was not offended.

He gave me a bored glance and went back to his drink

"I've been on the news" he mumbled.

"That's not it". I decided to be brazened. "I know: Becky's party. David, isn't it?"

He turned curiously and looked at me but a little blankly

"Don't you remember me?"

His eyes narrowed and his brow creased as he tried to remember. Then he gave me a rueful smile. "Sorry. Can you help me?"

In as much as he was giving off an I-would-really-love-to-be-alone vibe, yet his voice was very gentle and soothing. I wasn't going to let him get away without a fight.

"Alexis. Alexis Poe. Three years back"

"Three years? There's been a lot of parties since then" He said

"Well…" I thought about it and decided to jog his memory a bit, with the danger of belittling myself even before the conversation had started. "I came onto you so strong and had to be thrown out of the party" I shrugged. There! I said it. "That Alexis. The story ran for such a long time …" I noticed it was not ringing a bell. I didn't know how to take that. Was it that he didn't consider the incident such a bad one, that he had forgotten (which was quite noble) or was it that he didn't consider me important, that he had forgotten the incident?

"A lot of girls had made mistakes on my account" He swallowed sadly and went for his drink. "It is nothing I care to remember. Sorry"

Number two then; great.

But then my professional mind was triggered.

Something had happened to this all fun-loving Mr nice guy. Something really big by the look of it. Something that has totally changed him. If not, c'mon!! I wasn't bad looking (and that is putting it modestly), dressed to kill, in a playboy hotel and I was coming onto him. How disciplined can a guy be?

"Want to talk about it?" I tried

He looked at me curiously. "Talk about …?"

"It's obvious you are down. Want to talk about it?" I smiled. "It's my job and I'm good at it"

He chuckled sadly. "No"

"I cost more than £100 an hour in therapy sessions and I'm offering you the service free of charge and –"

He interrupted me in a polite but very hurtful way. "I'm sorry, miss …." He had already forgotten my name. "I just came to have a quiet drink. Can I?"

That cut me in the heart. My expression went wooden. I glared at him. Then I nodded, finished my drink in a gulp and left the bar and headed back to my room. As I entered the elevator, I noticed he had sighed in despair and was staring at me. The elevator doors swished shut.

II

The sun was setting on the horizon when I stepped out again and lay by the pool soaking the dissipating evening glow and warmth, my eyes closed. I had a thing about not staying angry too long. Nobody was worth the effort. I prided myself on that. I had forgotten the incident of the afternoon and was toiling with the idea of a young man coming my way and what I would do to him, when a silhouette fell over me. I opened my eyes.

"I've been looking for you all day" David said. "I wanted to apologize for this afternoon"

I stared at him.

"I really do apologize. It had nothing to do with you – "

"Of course it had nothing to do with me"

He smiled ruefully. "I'm really sorry"

There was an awkward silence as he expected a response which I wasn't ready to give. I just stared at him.

"Can I buy you a drink?" He tried. "Please" He signalled the waiter. Then he sat beside me and sighed. The waiter came over. "What would you like?"

I still stared at him. Suddenly, all he had put me through made me so cross.

"Lemonade" He whispered to the waiter. "Two glasses". As the waiter left he turned to me. "You really caught me at a bad time. I am really sorry. If you knew what I've been through ... if you were in my shoes ..." He looked away. "I'm not the kind of guy to get close to. I'm not worth it"

I studied his face and my heart melted again. "Are you alright?"

He nodded. "Yeah"

"Want to talk about it?"

"It's a long story"

"In case you haven't noticed, I am in a hotel with no date and nothing else to do for the next five days"

"You must have read something in the news sometime"

"Not really. I have been so busy these past few years; I've lost touch with the world. This is my first holiday"

He thought for a long time, I thought he was going to change his mind. The waiter came and left. He took a sip of the lemonade then looked at me.

"Let's go somewhere quiet" He said

"Wow. That serious, huh"

He didn't answer. He led me into the hotel to a quiet patio over-looking lovely scenery of the moors. We settled and started sipping our lemonade quietly. He then sighed and started talking:

III

It is pertinent to note here that my personal thoughts and words amidst his story are the ones in italics. Just so I don't confuse you.

"I will give you a little background. It will help you understand better the reasons that led me into this predicament" *he said.* "I come from quite a comfortable background"

You don't say.

"I had the good fortune of studying Law in Oxford and distance learning IT programming in Regent University. While I was doing that, I developed a programme that came to the notice of Google. They bought it for 12 million pounds"

Wow!!

He nodded. "Yeah. I was financially independent before I was 25. I practiced law for two years before my father died and I took over his Shipping Company. By the time I was 29, I had the world at my feet."

You can say that again

"So what happened? Did you run the business down?" I asked

"On the contrary" *He said.* "I doubled the assets of the company and increased my portfolio by 25%. I was richer than batman and Iron man put together"

He must have noticed my shocked expression.

"Figuratively, I mean". *He chuckled.* "I guess you could say I had my head screwed on straight" *He sighed* "The problem was that I have never lacked anything. My father gave me the best of everything. Then I came into money myself and my businesses have all been successful. I was in my juvenile prime. I could get anything I damn well pleased. Beautiful women of all manner were at my beck and call. I had no worries in life. I had what other people only dreamed about. I was the life and soul of every party. Authorities knew me. I was into international law. The Government consulted with me. The chief of Met police addressed me by my first name. Politicians invited me to their get-togethers. The celebrities wanted to associate with me. Bottom line: life was too easy, it became quite boring. I couldn't handle the boredom. I just couldn't. If I wasn't a balanced person, I might have resorted to … bad things … self-destructive bad things … suicide" *His eyes dropped* "I thought about it. But I don't have the heart for such stuff". "Instead I resorted to adventures. Something to excite me at least once a week; anything at all. I travelled the world; did all manner of stuff; got drunk; did sky diving; gambled; I even went into some deep jungle in the Brazilian amazon once in search of knowledge. That crazy. Came back from that with migraines and occasional blackouts. Said I wouldn't be doing that again" *He chuckled.*

"Did you do drugs?" I asked

"I said I didn't want to destroy myself. I was bored. Not crazy"

I smiled my gladness he had not done drugs

"I had four friends with the same background as I" *He continued*: "Sani, Ken, Mike and Brill. Very best friends. Our friendship developed after I formed these charities that went global for humanitarian purposes, going into war-torn places and helping out the oppressed; every now and then engaging with the armed forces and sponsoring stuff that the government could not do, that sort of thing; helps to encourage our guys that someone appreciates, you know. I think my friends liked what I was doing. We had acquiescence into countries that most people didn't have due to my knowledge of law and my connections"

He stalled and looked into space as if a memory just flooded back. Then he sighed and gave a mirthless smirk and continued:

"Sani was the tough strong-willed one. He was from one of the affluent class families in Kuwait. Though he had lived all his life in London. He was very passionate about anything he believed in. Brill was the only one who could challenge him. He was afraid of no one. Jamaican. Grew up in the rough neighbourhood of east

London, against all odds to break into the financial industry. His crisp decisions made him rise astronomically in the corporate world. By the age of 30, he was a director earning five figures and an authority in bank investments. Mike was the complete gentle man and peace lover. Anytime things got heated among us, which were quite often, he was the one that never took sides. His goals were only to maintain peace and friendship. He was the best of us, character wise; intelligence, you name it. He was a statistician that took over his father's business and made it into an empire over five years. Then he hired directors and worked from home".

These people make it sound so easy

"Then there is Ken. His whole life was one single purpose. Make wealth. If anyone was not a building block or a stepping stone towards achieving that, he had no time for you. He was a bit of a cryonic individual. But when he wanted to, he was the best company you could ever have. He was that kind of guy. It was no surprise he built his father's business into an Estate management empire covering the whole country. I did everything with them – girls, parties, surfing, bungee jumping, you name it. I also had four steady girlfriends beside my once in a while flings"

He must have noticed my face because he added

"I have everything. Shoot me"

"They know about one another?" I asked

"No. Best for everyone if we kept it like that, don't you think?"

Then he continued "They also were from my class of the society. As a matter of fact, all the girls I dated were from my class of the society or striving to be, you know what I mean. They were all soft, soppy, weak, synthetic, you know; the real definition of a lady – with long nails, painted faces and full of women liberation"

I laughed. Not because of what he said, but the way he said it. You wouldn't understand unless you were there.

"All except one. She lacked finesse" *He sighed.* "Tanya was rough"

"How do you mean?"

He looked at me. "Let's say I didn't always look forward to closing the shades with her"

I chuckled. I understood that. Hope you do because I'm not explaining it.

"Soon I wanted to explore a different kind of woman. The woman at the other extreme: raw, low societal class, maybe strong but definitely unsynthetic. A realistic woman who had seen the real suffering of life and has dealt with it. Someone who life had thrown everything at and she took it all in her stride and it did not destroy her or damage her psyche. Someone quite calm and down to earth. Someone different"

"Someone like Tanya"

"Tanya had not experienced the downside of this world. She was just rough. And could be volatile sometimes. There was always a seething energy with her. Everything must be her way or the world explodes... that kind of person. Someone who grew up with the world revolving around her"

Ah! I knew that type.

"That's not what I meant. I meant a woman who had seen the real world but still remained sweet and gentle and matured and approachable and welcoming ... you know: genuine. Someone like that"

"They are everywhere. All you had to do was look" I said

"I did look. They were not there. What you find are people who put up a front; a mask; political showcasing while underneath there is this murky mess that reeks of hypocrisy; a sense of entitlement; the world owes you and must pay. Everything has to be the way you want it; if not there is a problem. This is the way you are expected to be, or talk, or act. Herd mentality. Nothing true". *He sipped his drink.* "You can only pretend for so long. When the mask drops, it's not a pretty sight. I saw through the smiles; the sweet talks and the attempts to be societally acceptable. I saw through it all. My fantasy girl could not be found. I searched. From one picnic to another; one club or party to the next. My friends, who by the way were in on the adventure seeking refuge, helped me to search. We couldn't find my fantasy girl"

"But they knew about your four girlfriends?"

"How do you think I ended up with four girlfriends?"

"Oh" I mauled that over. "So they knew you were still searching?"

"It was an adventure. We were seeking new experiences. Life was boring. Really boring" As *he lifted the glass of drink to his lips, he muttered* "We were not going to commit suicide" *Then he took a long swig.*

I stared at his pensive look wondering if I should say something

"Why would boredom make you think of harming yourself"

He looked at me. "When there is nothing to strive for, you will be surprised the kind of thoughts that drop into your mind. The vices you tend to develop. The needs that gnaw at you, deep inside, trying to envelop you" *He sighed.* "You have no idea"

He paused for a long time brooding

"So?" I asked

"So what?" He broke out of his thoughts

"Is this too hard?" My psychiatrist instinct kicking in. "You want to talk of something else?"

He sighed and gave me a smile. "Nah. I will continue. Have to tell someone sometime. I don't know why but I'm comfortable with you"

I broke into a wide smile. Why? I don't know.

"So who were the two people you came into the hotel with?" I asked trying to kick start the story again

"That's my story. I'm getting into it now"

IV

"It all started one Friday morning. I had just finished my daily routine in the office of signing documents, making deals, affirming contracts and doing payments, those sorts of things, when my personal assistant, Florence informed me that Sani called and requested a call back. Sani was always full of fun plans and if he was calling on a Friday morning, that meant we are in for a shindig. I was excited. I called him back at once.

'Hey Sani; what's up?'

'Fish man! Just an update on the travel. I've booked for us to stay at the Four Seasons, Burj Alshaya. It's the best. Trust me'

'Oh! I trust you mon ami. You have the finest taste. I'd leave all the plans with you. Just tell me when to get ready' I said excitedly

'Remember; don't go yapping to the girls where we are going. We are soiling our royal oaths alright. The secret should die with us' He said

I busted into laughter. 'You can count on me. Promise'

'Clear your desk by the end of next week. We leave in two weeks' He said

'I will. See you later, man'

'Later, fish man' and Sani cut the line.

I smiled contentedly and made to stand up when Florence came into the office and informed me that all my girlfriends called in saying they were engaged for the weekend and could not make it over. Now that was my role – saying I wasn't available to three so I could spend time with one. I rotated them"

"Florence wasn't one of your girlfriends?"

"Florence?" *He chuckled* "She didn't even see me as a man"

Good for her!

"But she knew about the girls?"

"She's my PA. Sue me. I pay her a hefty salary to organise my life. What's it to you?"

I smiled.

"I have this foundation I run in the police department because of the rapport they had with my father. The whole police department had benefitted from it at one time or the other, I think. I don't know. On summer holidays, the charity usually organizes some kind of ball or gala where financial rewards are given to standout staff or their family. It is something they look forward to and I am glad to do. But because of it I have to go into the department every now and then for visits. You know, just to have an overview of what the needs might be for that year. I had gone there that morning to see the chief. As we sat chatting, there was a buzz in the main hall. I looked. Policemen were clapping as detectives led some young men in handcuffs into the building alongside a little teenage girl. A female detective had her arm around the little girl's shoulders as they walked in"

'What's going on?'

'Team 7. They just cracked a case. They are bringing the perps in' the chief said

I was impressed. I wanted to know more.

'Scarcity of jobs; get rich quick syndrome; whatever the excuse is. But this gang had been terrorizing folks around East London' The Chief said

'Drugs?'

'Kidnapping'

'Kidnapping!!' I was shocked. That was a new one in England.

'Yeah. We had to quell it fast before a wave begins'

I was relieved. You never knew where you could find yourself in the name of adventure and become a potential target. 'Did they ever kill anyone?'

He looked at me. 'Yes. Two'

My heart sank. 'Why?'

'If you call their bluff, they didn't take it kindly'

'But if you paid ...?' I was desperate

'Don't worry son. They've been caught. You don't have to be scared' He said soothingly

I'm not into the rough stuff. It scares me. I'd rather watch them in movies. But I had the utmost respect for these guys that faced it every day. That's why I maintained the foundation with gladness. A way of saying 'thanks for keeping us safe'.

'My lead detective is coming now to give me his reports' the chief concluded.

The lead detective walked in. He was a bald headed black guy in his forties. Quite fit with a reassuring smile"

"The man with the lady, I saw you with this morning?" I asked "He's a cop?"

He nodded and continued.

"'I believe you've met Sergeant Alfred' the chief said

'You won the award last year, didn't you?' I said smiling and shaking his hand gratefully.

'My team did. They work hard' He said decorously.

'Alfred's team is one of the best we have. They always close cases' The Chief said

Alfred turned to the chief and handed over a file. 'My report sir'

'How did it go?' the chief asked

'Her instincts were on the mark. She saved the girl' Alfred said

The chief thought briefly. 'But we can't encourage these spontaneous bursts. Someone could get hurt'

'Well,' Alfred shrugged. 'It is spontaneous bursts like this that has always closed cases. She somehow knows when to move with nothing but a hunch. You need to see her in the field...'

As they talked, I looked across the hall. There was only one 'her' in their team. She was being congratulated alongside her team mates while the culprits were being taunted by the other police staff. One of the culprits spat at the female detective. Before anyone could blink an eyelid, she had stepped up to the culprit and planted an explosive head-butt in his nose-bridge breaking it at once. The impact made me flinch and build saliva in my mouth. I swallowed.

'... But I understand what you are saying, cap. I will try and keep her on a leash' Alfred concluded staring into the hall, obviously embarrassed by what had just happened

The uniformed policemen hurriedly took the culprits away as her team members restrained her from doing any more damage, trying to calm her down. The parents of the girl appeared from an inner room so the detective calmed down trying to comport herself. She watched the child run into their arms and they all start to weep. The parents looked up and their eyes were full of gratitude to the female detective. She nodded to them, looking embarrassed at being gushed over, and walked over to her table and picked up a file. Then I saw her clearly. She had a plain solemn look with shades of healed patches of injuries on her face. Her long hair was tied aggressively back in a ponytail, revealing a smooth forehead. There was nothing attractive about her in any way except if you were into the hatchet outlook of female athletes. I am not. But the respect I had for Alfred was doubled in her. She is a woman for crying out loud. And she dodges bullets for a living. C'mon! You gotta be amazed at that. This one didn't look like she needed a man to protect her in anyway. Not pleasing to the eye ... but intimidating in a pleasant sort of way. I can't explain it. But that was the kind of vibe I got from observing her do her job"

"Well, I thought the lady I saw this afternoon with Alfred was very beautiful. But that's my opinion" I said.

"Potato, po-tar-to. Everyone has their taste. She wasn't mine" *He said*

"Fair enough. We go by your taste" I said

He looked at me, probably trying to ascertain if I was being sarcastic.

I chuckled.

"Don't disrupt the flow" *He said*

I chuckled and said "Sorry. I will not. Please continue"

He nodded still giving me the suspicious look.

I smiled again to reassure him.

I must admit I was enjoying the slow pace he was introducing the story; the way he was painting the pictures. It was somehow sucking me in. I have listened to a lot of clients tell a story so this was kudos to him. He had an intriguing way of engaging you in a discussion and –

Okay. I admit. I was still smitten by him. Sorry. But I was enjoying the story as well.

"Alfred and the Chief finished talking and Alfred nodded his excuse to me and left the room.

'Wow; that was a bit intense' I said, chuckling uncomfortably

The chief sighed. 'Sorry you had to see that. Alfred's second in command'

'The Lady?'

'Yeah. Clara. Some kind of a loose cannon. Always under the eye of Internal Affairs. Like what just happened. Someone is going to write a report soon. I'm just worried she's gonna pull the force into disrepute someday'

'But Alfred said she's always getting the job done' I contended

'Yeah; why do you think I'm 'just' worried?' He sighed and pulled the file to himself.

I took the cue and decided it was time to go back to my world of sane peaceful people. So I excused myself, promised to drop in again soon and left his office. The cops knew me and I might add, liked me. A few of the female cops have been a bit overenthusiastic in the past. Two once pulled me into an inner room on a charity day, one of them saying she had dreamed of this for a long time. I will leave it at that.

That is absolutely fine by me

So as I walked into the main hall, everyone was greeting and smiling. Alfred's team looked up and started waving. All but the lady detective. She was still reading her file. That intrigued me. I know women never look through me. That this plain-looking tomboy does, was really impressive. So I walked over to their table.

'Hey guys; congrats on your case. The chief told me'

All five guys smiled brightly and acknowledged my felicitations. The girl did not even look up. I gave a wry grin.

'Say; if you guys aren't doing anything this weekend, I have tickets to a good club that will do you all a nice bit of good'

'Rich boys' club? No Mr Reynolds' one of the boys said. Mathew was his name, I think.

'C'mon' I said smiling 'That's why I have the tickets. It's a hot club in Soho. Strictly by tickets. You would love it. My tickets give you VIP treatment. Free drinks, free snacks, the works' And I pulled out a wad of tickets to this club I was a shareholder in and started to distribute them. They all broke into these wide grateful grins. I pushed a ticket towards her. She did not look up. 'Detective; there is one for you as well. You can have a private room experience if you want. If it is available, they will give it with this ticket'

She looked up into my eyes. She has these illuminate emerald green eyes that seemed out of place in her plain injury shaded face that hit you like a shock. You blinked when you saw them. I blinked.

Would be amazing during aggressive interrogations. No wonder she was good at her job. She was made for this kind of life.

So, that's what it was. I knew the girl I saw had an unnerving beauty that gave her this picture of strength but I could not place my finger on what it was that made her striking.

So, that's what it was.

'No thanks' she said quietly and promptly went back to her reading.

The atmosphere was suddenly affected. Her colleagues stared at her. They were either angry she blew me off or worried she was playing with fire blowing me off. That gave me courage.

'Is there something you don't like about me, detective?' I asked

She looked up again and those emerald green eyes stared into mine.

'Maybe I can change' I added a bit hastily.

She thought for a second or so.

'No' she said blandly and went back to her reading.

Alfred tried to salvage the situation 'Don't take it personally sir. She is like that with everyone. It's a miracle she even has friends in this station'

'Friends?' Mason, another one said

'Colleagues, sir. That's what she has' Owen said.

'It's alright' I said and smiled. It was still a surprise to me.

And me

I mean, I have not had any brushes with her in my life. Where was the aggression coming from?

'Let me have the ticket sir' Alfred said and glaring at her, said 'I'm sure she would like to go'

I gave it to him, smiled my goodbye and headed for the door.

'What's the matter with you?!' I heard Alfred snarl

'Yeah! What's wrong with you?' Luke, one of the other boys asked

She just glanced up at them briefly and went back to her reading.

I smiled to myself realizing that not every woman I met wanted to have something to do with me.

I headed back to my office to finish my day.

V

I was walking into the office when my mobile rang. I stopped and sat on Florence's table to answer it.

'What's the news Kenny?'

Ken laughed. 'How are you doing, Mon ami? Are you taking any of your girls to the party? If it's not Deidre, I'm not coming with mine. I don't want to be answering awkward questions'

'What are you on about? What party?'

'What do you mean "what party"? The Party'

'What party?'

'Why don't you look at your diary, Sméagol'

I looked at Florence who showed me the invitation card

'Oh! Becky's Party!! Of course!'

'You forgot, didn't you? I don't believe this guy. You gave her the club for a venue!!'

'I did? So I did. I forgot. C'mon. A lot on my mind!'

'Like what?'

Attempting to change that line of discussion, I declared 'I'm not taking any of my girls to that place. Becky's parties are not where you take your girlfriends to. Are you nuts?'

'Cool. I wanted to be sure' Ken said.

'What's the arrangement?'

'We are going with Sani's car. He will pick Mike and Brill. Then we'll come to your place. How's that?'

'Sold'

'So, no girlfriends?'

'No girlfriends' I confirmed

'And to think you forgot; you –'

'Bye Kenny' I cut him off and turned to Florence. 'And to think I was trying to arrange a weekend with one of them' I chuckled. 'The forces are always with me, eh'

'Be careful, sir' Florence said

I looked at her in *shock* 'What on earth do you mean?'

'You have four girlfriends. What else are you looking for going to a party without any of them?'

'They are the ones who are not around on a Friday night, Florence. Not me'

'Even if any of them were around, you still wouldn't have gone with her'

'How can you say such a thing?' And I left her and walked into my office.

VI

My friends and I stormed the party venue an hour after it had started. We were the life and soul of the party, so we liked to make an entrance. As usual with us, we were deep in non-politically correct arguments as we approached the entrance. Something about what ethnic group was overwhelming the NHS ... something like that. I don't even remember now; which was ridiculous because all of us had private healthcare insurance. We have never gone NHS. But that was the life of our friendship. No hard feelings.

The queue of people begging and trying to get in was like a Manchester United/Liverpool match. We usually skipped the lines. A lot of times we did that purposely. Hey; don't hate us for it. We are rich; we own the club and we are the life of the party. What more?

Becky's bouncers were busy. Two muscular dudes standing by the door maintaining order. Sani was in front sauntering towards the door. I was behind him still making my argument with Brill and Mike when I heard this sonorous velvety voice.

'I need to see your pass, sir'

Sani had ignored the girl and was walking on. The girl grabbed his arm and brought him up short.

'I said I need to see your pass'

'Get your hands off me!!' Sani snarled. 'Are you insane?!!'

All of us turned in surprise.

That was when I saw her.

She was the one checking the tickets and validating the passes. She was seated. First thing that struck me was the way my heart skipped and started racing when I saw how beautiful she was. I didn't understand why initially. Hey; I'd seen beautiful girls in my time. But nothing like this. Then I realised what it was: I had fantasized about how I wanted my perfect woman to look like. And there she was sitting right across from me. It was like a déjà vu feeling. I knew at once she was new in town. How could I describe her? .... Have you seen the movie "Cutting Edge"? Old movie.

I shook my head

She had that Moira Kelly teenage look.

"I haven't seen it"

"What of the NCIS series?"

"Some of them"

"The ones with "Ziva David"?"

"No. I have not followed it that much"

"Oh! You need to see the ones with Ziva David when she was newly introduced. That kind of teenage intensity. Better still, have you seen the movie Alitha?

He had watched a lot of movies!!

"She had that kind of imposing presentation: Refreshing teenage beauty that exudes both innocence and confidence. Like she has never known sin; and yet you know she has. I can't explain it. It was breath-taking. Her dark rich hair was glistening in the moon. There wasn't a single acne on her smooth supple face. When she validated your pass and smiled, it was as if the whole place lit up.

Goodness me!! How can a man describe a woman like that? I was green with envy as I wondered how he would describe me to someone else. I needed to watch Alitha for some reason

I took all these in at a glance.

The two bouncers were approaching hurriedly

'Do you just talk to anyone you see?! What are you, stupid?! Don't you have common sense?! We walked past the line, bitch!! What does that tell you?!!'

The girl heaved herself up.

'Wow' Mike whispered

And rightfully so because under the fresh teenage look was a six-foot amazon. Her curves would win any miss world contest. Her awesome flat tummy made her streamlined bosom look like they were propping her polo shirt up. She was a hair's breadth shorter than Sani and as she dramatically stood up, Sani swallowed in surprise but kept his posture. She had on a skirt that was slightly above the knees. Her legs were long, straight and full. I have never seen such completeness in beauty before in my life. It was un-canny. Among my fantasies I had imagined a woman so complete in beauty. I never knew she existed. I was glued.

She stared at him, her face creased in curiosity. 'It tells me you like looking for trouble' she said in her quiet sonority.

Sani's face went pugnacious and he menacingly swayed towards her as the bouncers interceded. She had not moved.

'Sorry Mr Rasheed!' One of the Bouncers blundered, coming be-tween them.

'What's wrong with you?' The other snarled at the girl. 'That's the boss!!'

Her expression softened when he said that. She opened her mouth and it looked like she wanted to apologise.

'She is new in town, Mr Rasheed. She doesn't know how it works around here' the first bouncer was saying.

'Oh. Hey...' She was saying gently

'I want her out of here. Make it happen. Do you hear' Sani piqued

'Easy, Sani. Calm down' I said, smiling reassuringly.

Just then Becky came to the door. 'My boys!! You made it!!' And she hugged Sani, who did not reciprocate. She then saw the faces of all my friends. They were all solemnly glaring at the girl. 'What's wrong?'

'Do you just let anybody into these premises, Becky?' Brill asked and walked on into the club

Becky was exasperated. 'What's going on?'

Sani dragged his eyes away from the girl and walked on. Ken followed.

'Wow' Mike said again as we walked in leaving Becky perplexed. These parties were important to her and her business contacts.

'How beautiful she was?' I asked expectantly

'Beautiful?' Brill grimaced

'Are you nuts?' Ken completed

Mike stared at me strangely. I realized I was alone in my perceptions of her. That didn't bother me. My friends were the average hypocritical citizens of this country. One person runs something down, and the rest of the crew follow suit without stopping just once to think for themselves. Yeah; I was used to it.

I looked back towards the door and saw Becky discussing with one of the bouncers

'Your friend insulted the bosses …' he was saying before the music in the party drowned out his voice.

We mingled with the party, but I couldn't help myself. I wanted to see more of this amazing fantasy-come-to-life. I soon detached from my friends and the party and grabbing a drink, I moved to a vantage point by the bar to watch the door. I was waiting to see when she would come into the hall. Becky was saying something to her, and her head was down. I wondered what she was telling her.

'So, you seriously think this amazon is beautiful?' Mike had come behind me and noticed what I was looking at.

'What did you mean by "wow"?' I asked

'You know how intimidating Sani can be' Mike said.

I nodded

'She was not afraid. I have not seen that in anyone before. And definitely not in a girl. That really surprised me'

I thought I was the only one that noticed. She was beautiful and she was confident. Not the facial beauty related confidence that bothers on shallowness and pride. No. This was an innate confidence. This lady believed she could handle anything. She was ticking all my boxes. I became excited.

Becky must have said something. She nodded sadly and walked off into the night. Becky re-joined the party. I turned to the barman.

'A bottle of champagne and two glasses please' I said.

'Don't tell me you are going after her' Mike mused

'Whatever gave you that idea?' I grabbed the bottle and glasses and hurried out of the door. Mike shrugged and went back to the party.

.   *   *

She was sitting quietly on the hood of a car staring into the night. It was a cold night but she didn't seem to be feeling it in her polo shirt. She was absolutely still. I had a jumper and jacket on. I removed the jacket as I approached her.

'Are you worried your friends hurt my feelings?' She asked while I was two cars away behind her. She didn't even turn

I stalled in surprise.

'How did you know it was me?' I asked as I came close.

She looked at me and gave a slight demure smile 'Your perfume'

'My perfume? You picked out my perfume in the midst of everyone else's?'

'I noticed everyone else's as well'

'That's remarkable' I raised the Jacket towards her shoulders 'May I?'

She gave me her shoulders 'That's really kind of you'

'It's my privilege' I said draping the jacket over her shoulder

'Thank you' she smiled.

'So what's the name of my perfume?' I asked

'The Night from Frédéric Malle' she said promptly and noticed my surprise and smiled. 'Customized fragrance. Has a gentle rich ambiance. Not aggressive to the nose. Must have cost you a lot or you must be on first name basis with Dominique Ropion'

My goodness!! She was right on the money. It was exclusively prepared in Turkey. Cost me a pocket.

I stared at her. 'Wow. You know your perfumes'

'I know a lot of things' She said and smiled

I was awed. The way she talked... the confidence that exuded from her ... there was no pride. No showing off. No need to impress. Just a calm confidence. A touch of – there was nothing petty about me. I can't explain it.

'My name is David'

She stared into my face for a long second as if she was trying to memorize my face or my name. Her eyes were soft as if she was pleased about something. 'What are you doing here David? You should be in the party. Enjoying yourself'

'So should you' I said

'No. I don't do crowd. Why do you think I volunteered to help out at the door instead?'

'So what are you doing here then?'

'Helping out my friend. Becky is my friend'

'Was she telling you off?'

She smiled and sighed 'Yeah. Sorry I grabbed your friend's arm. I was just doing my job'

'That's nothing. Don't worry about it. At least it made you come out here. A chance for me to speak with you' I said

She stared at me, a muted smile on her lips and the softness still in her eyes.

'Can I sit with you?' I asked

She kept staring at me

'I brought champagne' I added

The smile broadened. 'I can't drink. Alcohol makes me misbe-have'

'oh.' I leaned on the car beside her. 'I wouldn't want that'

She looked at me surprised. 'You wouldn't want that? That's a first'

We observed each other. She seemed to study my disposition maybe trying to ascertain the kind of person I was

'Can I sit?' I asked again

She still stared at me, the slight smile on her lips

'I just want to talk' I confirmed

'Talk?' She asked

'I'm more interested in getting to know you than anything hap-pening in that party'

She kept the muted smile and soft look. 'Why?'

We observed each other.

'Mr Reynolds!'

We broke stare and I turned towards the voice. It was Alfred and his crew.

'You made it!' I said and we shook hands

'Just got here. Thanks for this, sir' Alfred said

The rest gave their greetings as I smiled with joy that they came

'Enjoy. You are the most important people there as far as I'm con-cerned'

They smiled. Then Clara came into the light as she walked by.

'You finally made it' I said, smiling

She shrugged and walked on

'Don't push it Mr Reynolds. I had to threaten her to come' Alfred said

I laughed and gave him the bottle of champagne. 'This might calm your frail nerves. It hasn't been opened'

Alfred nodded his thanks and they waved their 'see you soon' and left.

'Definitely' I replied as they walked away

'You have an amazing effect on people' the girl beside me said

'No I don't'

She chuckled. 'I noticed how everyone in the queue stared as you came close'

'They always do that. We own the place'

'Not all of you. The girls in particular, stared at YOU. I saw'

'You see a lot' I said.

She chuckled. 'I do' Then she stood up. 'I want to take a walk'

'Okay' And we strolled off.

I don't know how long we strolled but somehow there was an aura about this girl that made me content just walking silently beside her and looking at the moon. But at a point I tried to start a conversation again.

'Say, I am really sorry about how my friends treated you' I tried

She smiled. 'I know' And she kept walking.

'You don't talk much, do you?'

'I do. When I have something to say'

'Are you alright with me walking with you? I'm not boring you in any way?'

She shook her head. 'Your company is very comforting. Thanks'

'No, thank you'.

'Do you respect every woman like this?'

'I don't know what you mean' I said coyly

She smiled and fell silent again. I kept glancing at her as we walked. She seemed so serene; I felt it was unfair to interfere with her tranquillity. But at some point I really started to get uncomfortable with the quietness, feeling like I really was not being a good company.

'I feel awkward just walking beside you like this' I finally said

She smiled. 'You can talk. I will listen. I love to listen'

I thought about it. 'I don't know what to talk about. I hardly know you'

'What would you like to know?'

'Are you new in town?'

'Have you seen me before?'

'No'

'Then I'm new in town'

I chuckled. She smiled and looked at me. Her eyes still had that softness and I could not explain why but it made me feel very good. 'Okay.' I thought for a while. 'I don't know what else to ask you'

'You don't have to ask me anything. You can just talk to me' She said

I thought about that. 'I don't know what interests you'

'What interests you?' She asked

I really wanted to impress her that I felt lost for words about what to discuss. I chuckled and shrugged in embarrassment.

'What kind of work do you do?' She asked, obviously trying to help me out.

'Boring stuff. I hardly think it will interest you'

'Try me. You'd be surprised'

I smiled. 'I'm a courier for exports and imports'

I waited for the blank confused look and obvious question every other girl asks.

She only nodded and smiled. 'That's very lucrative; and if I might add, interesting'

'You know what that means?' I asked in surprise

'You own ships'

I almost jumped up in joy. This was the first girl that I didn't have to explain my job to after that ambiguous introduction. This lady was impressing me by the minute.

'You seem impressed I said that'

'You read faces too?' I asked, awestruck. 'Is there anything you cannot do?'

She chuckled in that velvety voice. 'So, do you always throw parties every Friday night?'

'Not me. My friends and I always get invited to parties every Friday night. It's like we are the stamp of approval that a party is worth attending in these parts'

'You must be very important'

'I don't know about that, but a lot of people love to associate with us. Most of them are not friends in the real sense of it. Just people looking for a business connection or a favour or an opportunity to lift their CV ...' my voice tapered off because I noticed the smile on her face froze and her soft eyes went granite. Something was wrong. I enquired with my eyes. She raised a finger across her lips to signify silence while her eyes surveyed the environment. That was when I noticed where we were: we had turned into and walked deep into a dark alley with no CCTVs. It was quiet and dank.

I didn't understand why she was going paranoid. 'What's wro –'

'Shh!!' She turned towards the entrance. 'We shouldn't be here' and she headed for the entrance at once. I followed.

From the shadows, two figures appeared. We froze. As we wanted to withdraw backwards, we suddenly noticed that two had appeared behind us. My heart started to thump. I knew what this meant. How did we get into this? I forgot the neighbourhood I was in. There was a reason it was called a red-light district apart from the obvious.

'Hello maties; missed your way?' One of the yobs asked

I pushed the girl behind me as they came close. I could smell the alcohol, sweat and tobacco. They could smell our perfumes...

One sniffed 'Rich kids'

'What on earth are you doin 'ere?' The main one asked

'We made a mistake. We are on our way now' I said and made to move

He stood in my way. 'It will cost ya'

'What do you want?' I asked

'What do ya' ave?' He asked

I grabbed my wallet. 'I have –'

He snatched it from me and pulled out the notes inside and tossed the wallet aside.

'Can we go now? Please?' I asked

'Of course' He stepped aside.

'Thanks' And as I moved, they stopped the girl.

'Only you' He said

I stared at him in horror

'Trade the girl' He said

My heart sank 'What?'

'Just walk on. Don't even look back'

'I can't do that. She is with me. I can't leave without her. Please'

'I said walk on'

With my heart banging against my side, I stood my ground. 'Please'

'I said "walk – on"' He grated, moving menacingly towards me

I suddenly felt claustrophobic. Somehow, I knew death was nearby. 'Please' I said, hardly recognizing my own voice.

He grabbed my shirt in a steely vice grip and as he pulled me close, I saw the glint of a knife briefly before he stabbed. I closed my eyes in anticipation.

I felt nothing.

It happened in such a blur, but this is what I saw: I opened my eyes and saw him looking at me in shock. He was wincing. I looked down. The girl had grabbed his wrist with the blade one inch from my ribs. She had twisted the wrist and must have been doing something to that hand that I could not see but the yob was wincing and grunting all at the same time. In a split second, his legs were swept off the ground. As he crashed heavily on the ground, he took me with him. Her hands moved in flashes as the other yobs attacked. One crashed against bins. One cracked his head on the brick wall and the other sprawled so dangerously I thought he had broken his neck. One last crack at the first one as he made to stand. He grunted, his eyes unfocused and he slumped in a heap. I was panting and staring in shock. She rushed to me and helped me up.

'Are you alright?' she asked earnestly

I stared, speechless.

'You're alright. Walk. Now' And she was already moving

I stood rooted staring around at the yobs writhing on the ground. 'How did you –'

 'David!!' She hissed and waved savagely at me to come on. I ran after her still awed. 'When they stand, we are in trouble'

And sure enough I heard a roar behind me. I looked. The yobs were getting to their feet and pointing. She slapped my shoulder and took off. I ran after her shocked at her speed. Gosh; this girl could run!

Who was this girl? This enigma? My goodness!

We were on the high street in a moment.

'Taxi!!' I roared at a black cab.

She turned and ran back to me as I bundled into one.

'Where to, sir?' The man asked

'Just go!! Go!! Go!!' I cried

'Where do I go?!' He snarled irritatingly

The yobs turned the corner, scanning the environment, studying the crowd's body movement.

'I have to switch on the metre' the driver continued

I noticed the yobs start to approach.

'Switch it on!! Just go!!' I cried

The yobs started running towards us, pointing and snarling.

'I don't want any arguments when I ask for –'

The girl swung the car door and it slammed into the first yob to get to the car. He reeled backwards, destabilizing the others. The driver flinched in shock. The rest were trying to bundle into the windows. I squirmed into a seat, evading a clawing arm

'Gooo!!!' I roared

The girl parried away the knife wielding hand of another one. I don't know what she did, but the yob squirmed and fell on his knees as the cab screeched off into the night, the others falling away.

Hyperventilating, I stared behind me at the yobs that had stopped chasing and were cursing.

'Are you alright?' She asked me

I looked at her. Her face was calm but her eyes had intensity. I was speechless. I just stared in awe. This kind of women only existed in my fantasies. They were not real. Strong women did not look like the cartoon character Ladybug. They were never this beautiful. They were never feminine. There was always an unpresentable, attribute; some unfeminine disposition. Probably in their way of talking, smell of tobacco, bad teeth, coarse voice or at least their walk. They were never spotless, angelically beautiful, voice like a nightingale, smell of vanilla, waltz that gives an instant stirring in certain down stair quarters and character of a virtuous woman. They only existed in men's fantasies.

'Why would you do that?' Her voice broke into my thoughts.

I stared at her still unable to talk

'Is this just a habit with you? Standing up for people?! Sacrificing yourself?!' She sounded annoyed. 'Those men were about to kill you because of a girl you don't even know! Who does that?!!'

I was still staring at her in awe.

She suddenly leaned forward and crushed her lips on mine. And boy could this girl kiss. The warmth engulfed me completely. She held me tight for one minute, then suddenly pushed me away and turned her back on me, staring out of the window. My head was reeling. I could not think. What do I say? What do I do? This was strange quarters to me. I had never met someone so complete in my life.

I held her arms and she gave a sigh and looked at me. Her expression was broken as if she was fighting her impulse but knew in her mind she was losing the fight. I could see her chest heaving as she stared into my eyes. I could see her head telling her to say no but her supple lips were yearning. I didn't give the head anymore chance to think. I came close and her warm lips received me longingly. The same overwhelming envelope covered me again. Boy, this girl could kiss!!

We broke and stared into each other's eyes. Then we crushed into each other again, this time more fervently than the last.

'Let's go to my place' I panted when we broke

She stared at me through those glazed eyes, biting her lip

'Why?' she asked

I swallowed unable to think.

'Let's go to my place' I repeated

'Are you sure?' She panted back 'I know the rules'

And I did too. You never took a fling to your house especially when you had a serious relationship"

"'A' serious relationship?"

Okay! A number of serious relationships. Shut up, will ya?

"Serious relationships or not, this was no fling. This was different. I was falling fast for this enigma who had ticked all my boxes and then some, by the minute. This was so intense. Rationale was thrown out the window.

'I'm sure' I had said. 'Besides I need to pay the cabman'

She pulled out my wallet and money and handed them over. 'We don't need to go to your place'

How did she …? when did she …? I was thinking in my head because I was lost for words.

But I kept my composure and kept staring at her longing angelic face.

'We do' I said before we started kissing again oblivious of the taxi driver. It was a miracle he got us to the house in one piece. I don't even remember at what point I was able to give him my address.

.   *   *

We didn't speak again until we got to my house. As we entered the house, I locked the door and turned to usher her into the living room, but she was not interested in the least in my opulence. She didn't even look around. Her gaze was fixated on me. She pushed me against the door and crushed her lips on mine. We sank to the floor right there.

Safe to say, she was well versed in the skills of the ancient Indian arts.

I don't need to explain that now, do I?

This was how I have always fantasized to be taken which had never happened until that night. It had always been a usual routine of expected manoeuvres of which I literally took lead and did practically everything. Not this night. Without being graphic or inappropriate, I will put it this way: twice the throes of pleasure washed through me like never before that I tried to scream but could not. Once I heard my voice whimpering and I didn't recognize it as mine. She actually put a hand over my mouth at some point while still working me with such intensity. It was as if she had studied my body anatomy and physiology and really knew where all my pleasure nerve heads were. I was groaning apologetically, unable to raise a limb. I looked into her eyes at a point and saw softness and gratitude; like it meant a lot to her to make me happy. I had never seen that in a woman before. It sent goose bumps through me. And that is not what you want to happen to you when throes of pleasure are reverberating through your whole body. You would think life is about to end. Then at the crest of a climax that she controlled in me until she was ready, [I don't know how she did it], she let me go and my head could not take the rapturous euphoria. With white knuckled grab at the rugs, gasping, vibrating and dribbling, I blacked out.

Wow!!

My heart was racing. I didn't understand why. Wow.

WOW!!

VII

I woke up to the smell of eggs and bacon. I sighed and stirred. Then I sat up. I was still in the living room. My whole body ached but I felt so happy. I didn't understand it. I remember hazily partially waking up in the middle of the night and vaguely noticed her propping herself up with her elbow and looking at me with those same soft kind eyes. I had smiled and asked what she was looking at. She had smiled back and sighed but before she could reply, I had slept off again.

Or maybe it was a dream. I don't know

The sun rays were coming in through the blinds now. I wondered what time it was.

'Good afternoon' the sonorous whisper came from across the room. I turned. She was sitting on a stool by the door to the kitchen in my track suit. Without makeup she looked like a fresh teenager. My eyes involuntarily narrowed in veneration. I smiled. She smiled back. 'I hope you don't mind. I borrowed your track suit. I didn't want to look like a girl from the morning after'

'What time is it?' I asked

'About three in the afternoon'

'What?' I was horrified

'I already had breakfast and lunch. Yours is laid out in the dining if you can have them all' she said 'The tea is cold now, though'

She cooked?!

She cooked!!

She cooks!!

She knows how to cook!!!

I rested my case. I had nothing more to say about this damsel.

She kept semi-rotating on the stool. 'I had to wait for you to wake. I feel it's rude to leave without saying goodbye'

My heart did a summersault. The thought of her leaving ever again suddenly scared me. Now that scared me even more - the fact that I was thinking like this after just one night. It was uncanny. But like I said, rationale does not come into it when hormones and chemistry are in play.

Yes!! I was deeply besotted and a tad addicted and I knew it. You can't control these things.

'Goodbye?' I asked

She looked at me, her eyes enquiring but her face bored. 'Don't do that'

'Do what?'

'Don't tell me that suddenly you are infatuated. I'm the best you've ever had'

She was the best I have ever had!!!

And that's saying a lot, coming from me.

But in her humility she didn't even know it

'You don't even know me' she completed

'And I want to know you. Stay'

'You have a relationship don't you?'

I stalled and swallowed, the thought of comparing her to any of the others making me to grimace inside.

'Exactly what I thought' She concluded

'This is different' I blurted out

She was quiet for a second 'How?'

'I don't know. All I know is I don't want you to go'

She stared intently at me.

'Why not sleep it over. Your mind is a bit of a muddle right now. By tomorrow, your mind will be clearer' She finally said

'I can sleep it over with you right here' I contended

She gave a lopsided chuckle 'It will only complicate your life. You don't need that' then quietly she said 'You don't deserve it'

God! How does she do that? Show so much care in her eyes, it was amazing. It was as if she was saying I was too good for her. That all she wanted for me was good in all manner even if it involved her being sad. What woman does that?!

And what woman does that without saying a word?

'That is my problem' I hastily said 'Please stay'

She stared at me.

'Stay' I repeated, hoping my imploration will impact her somehow.

'What do you intend to gain from this?' She finally asked

'Why are you more concerned about my wellbeing than yours? Who does that?'

'I can take care of myself' she quietly said without an iota of smugness, it was intimidating.

'I know'. I admitted

Then I clambered laboriously to my feet and started making my way towards her, hoping I would achieve the feat. 'I have been with girls in my time. None thinks of my wellbeing more than theirs. Not one. Why are you doing that?'

Yes! I made it to her and stood between her legs and stared into her fresh face.

She looked into my eyes so intently, I felt my eyes drying. 'You are the kindest man I have ever met'.

This lady was driving me crazy!! This enigma. This fountain of beauty! This completeness in a woman. This materialization of fantasy! This embodiment of pleasure! This encapsulation of …

"*I get your point!*"

"Sorry. I just wanted you to get the picture of how I felt at that moment"

"*I got the picture at the party. Continue*"

Frankly, this mystery girl was beginning to irritate me. No girl is that good. If you think you are, write me an email…!

Okay, I'm jealous. Shoot me.

'Stay. Please' I tried. 'Let me get you out of my system' I chuckled uneasily.

'If I stay, you can't get me out of your system' that quiet voice warned me.

I thought about that for just a brief moment. 'I'll take my chance'. I was desperate to experience this girl for a while.

I know what you are going to ask. 'What about my four girl-friends?' 'What of the complications that will come with a live-in lover?' 'How could you be a successful businessman if your thoughts went like this?'

The obvious answer was: 'Beats me'. I wasn't thinking straight. Matters of the heart make a man very stupid.

"*My question is how were you able to have four girlfriends being as famous as you were and got away with it for so long and nobody told nobody*"

"I asked myself that same question a number of times. I didn't like the answers I got"

"*Which were…?*"

"Do you see me lying on your couch doc?"

"*Sorry*"

"Anyway, the enigma stared at me from under her eyelashes like a pleasant little girl curious about newly found information.

Then she sighed, smiled and looked away. 'I'll go and get my stuff'

'No need for that. I'll buy you anything you want' I said without thinking

She chuckled and when she chuckles, it's such a sight to see. 'I'll go and get my stuff'.

'I'll drive you'

'It's daylight. Are you sure you want to be seen together with me?'

'C'mon!!' I protested

She shrugged 'Okay'.

Then she headed towards the door.

I hurriedly grabbed a pair of trousers and a T-shirt and ran after her.

VIII

I was sitting in the car in the parking lot of the suburb where Becky lived when she briskly came stomping towards me. Enigma walked casually behind her holding a travel bag.

'What do you think you are doing, David?' Becky asked bending into the car 'What about your girl friends?'

I scratched my ears acknowledging the impending complications 'I know, Becky ... but this feels so right'

'It's not about how it feels, David. And you know it' Becky said. 'There are rules ... and you are about to break them'

'I can take care of myself'

'What about her? Who takes care of her? Are you going to play with her heart?'

'No!' I affirmed. 'Never. Listen Becky; this feels different. This feels genuine. I don't know. But from my point of view, this is genuine. We can weather any storm from the girls'

'And your friends?' Becky asked the inevitable question

'What about my friends?' I asked a little tightly

'What are they going to think?'

'It's none of their business'

'Really? What if they turn against you –'

'Why would they do that?' I interrupted, irritated and not knowing why

'What do you mean, why would they do that?!' Becky leaned in more so the girl would not hear what she was about to say, 'You have four girlfriends!' she hissed 'Everyone expects you to pick who you want from that pool – who you will be inviting home to your house. They are all your class'. She pointed through herself to signify the girl standing outside 'She is not your ilk. She is not your circle. She doesn't think the way you guys do'

'What do you mean by that?!' I quizzed getting more irritated. I have never liked condescending people. They leave a sour taste in my mouth.

I don't think that was what was irritating him.

'I don't like the way you are talking' I said.

She looked utterly shocked at my reaction as some truths hit her 'Do you even know who she is? Do you know anything about her? What's her name?'

I stared at her, no response coming into my mind. Knowing all I know now, I realize how stupid I must have looked in her eyes. Come to think of it, I didn't know her name. I didn't even know her name and I was taking a plunge. Wow!

But that was not the case on the day. Rather I let my irritation flow into my voice as I hissed back at her without letting the girl outside notice: 'Are you saying I should not trust you? She is your friend and you allowed her to stay in your house'

She slouched back as she knew the implications of my not trusting her. I had a foundation that solely patronized her business and like I said before, we had shares in all her doings. She sighed and then quietly said 'you should have asked me first before making this decision'

'It just happened. But then, we are adults and capable of knowing what is good for us. Don't you think?'

She nodded in a resigned manner, looked at me and stepped away from the car. She and the girl stared at each other.

'I will only go if I know I have your blessing' the girl said quietly

Becky glanced at me, and then turned to the girl 'You have my blessing'.

They hugged, pecked each other and Becky gave me a final glance and headed for her house and the girl joined me in the car.

'I'm sorry about that'

'That's expected', She said

I looked at her in admiration. She didn't even look upset.

'But you're okay with this?' I asked encouragingly

'I am okay with whatever you want. Like I said before, you are the kindest man I have ever met' and she smiled. All the clouds left the car. I smiled back and fired the ignition and we drove off.

IX

"And just like that, the most memorable, physical, sensual, blissful six days of my life started. At least, that was what it was supposed to be – six days. Turned out differently; but I'm getting to that.

I had travelled the world and had become bored with it; she did not want to go out much neither, so it fitted well. We spent the whole six days indoors, intimately exploring all fantasies I could imagine. I didn't even need to say it. Somehow, she just knew what I wanted. Fifty shades had nothing on us. She was insatiable. It was intense and fresh every day. I would wake up in the morning wondering what exciting thing would happen that day. I was like an expectant youth. Our role plays were some of the deepest secret fantasies I have ever had; I sometimes suspected she had read some of my teenage diaries. I was hooked so deep I was not thinking of anything else anymore except Enigma. The weekend was not enough for me, so I called Florence to manage the office and take all my calls while I worked from home.

Sometimes I would be lying on my rug working, and a shadow will fall over me. I would turn and see a dominatrix standing astride directly over my face just like I have always fantasized. The impact that had on me first time was so intense it gives me a headache right now just thinking about it. Sometimes the house will become so quiet because I have been working for a while. I will go looking for her, only to see her lying in a room dressed like a princess in distress waiting to be saved, tears and all. It was so believable it was empowering. I would rush and save her in all bravado like I had imagined if ever it happened. For gratitude, she would draw the curtains"

"Sometimes the games got a tad dangerous where she would ignore my safe word and stretch me just enough to the edge before drawing me back in. Sometimes I would pass out. Sometimes the pleasure will leave me speechless. Only staring and gasping for breath. Once, while still in our barest, she was trying to sort a malfunctioning gas-cooker out before we went upstairs and I grabbed her from behind, in an attempt to surprise her into submission. That day will forever be etched in my brain. She gave me a glimpse exhibit of her strength and unsettling skillset. She grabbed my wrists and slowly pulled apart my entwined fingers from her waist, turned around, locked my arms, rendering them useless for any offensive gestures and forced me struggling helplessly onto the sofa; pinned my arms down and sat astride me.

'Look at me' She whispered as she initiated her intensions. 'Don't look away. Don't close your eyes. Keep looking at me. Try and break free if you can. But keep your eyes on me'

I tell you, that was difficult. As she grinded me to a pulp, and the pleasure surged through my head, trying to maintain eye contact was the most difficult thing to do, especially as she kept pulverising the poor soul despite four intense rhapsodic climaxes and resuscitations. She maintained her valley-deep, intense rhythm, nonstop for one and a half hours, digging her nails into my wrists, gritting her teeth, hissing, whimpering and vibrating every few minutes. Yet she maintained the rhythm and never removed her gaze from my face, although her eyes blanked out every time she vibrated. Each stroke was deliberate and systematic, my whole being ebbing with each impact. Looking at the whole scene, being involved and sucked in completely, I felt like my head was about to explode. Tears ran down my cheeks and I was trembling. I was begging and the more I begged the more she increased the intensity of the grind. Just at the point of losing consciousness, my voice a mere rustle in my throat, she quaked again, gasped and gradually stalled. Then she sighed deeply, licked away the tears on my cheeks and gave me this intense slurping kiss. Then her soft intense eyes stared at me with such affection, I blushed. Her overwhelmingly innocent face smiled. My mind could not match her innocent and gentle demeanour to what just happened

'I'll let you be' She whispered, released my wrists and rolled away to have a shower.

Twenty minutes after she was done, I was still shivering and trying to get my brain to function again. The nerve ends all over my body were still screaming and waves of goose bumps kept sweeping through me. It was uncanny. I felt completely dominated, well ground and taken over.

On another day, when I came back to sanity, I looked at her, tears in my eyes and panted 'Didn't you hear the safe-word?'

'I did' She answered quietly her soft eyes fixed on me

'You could have killed me' I whined, my voice tinged with alarm.

'But I didn't' She had said, stroking my chest gently, her intent eyes never leaving my face.

There was this overwhelming envelope of feeling that I could not explain. A mixture of pleasure, sensuality, passion, warmth and fear. It is hard to explain. It was dangerous. You knew it was dangerous but yet you wanted it more and more every day. It was as if she was taking over my very soul, and she knew it.

She just stared at me with that angelic gaze, slight demure smile and soft eyes.

'Do you trust me?' She asked.

She always asked that. And every time she did, I felt a bit more of her take over me. The feeling was …. The feeling was….

He sighed and seemed to drift away for a split second. Then he chuckled mirthlessly "Did you know there was a lot you could do with yoghurt or ice cream that made a man stay longer than he intended to?"

"Explain that"

"I am not even going to try" "Just be rest assured all my fantasies and that of everyone I know have been spent. There is nothing anybody can do now that will be new to me or come to think of it, impress me"

He drifted again briefly "Nothing".

This lady was dangerous!!

This lady was dangerous with a capital "D"!!

This lady was a malignant parasite that needed irradiation!! Such girls should not be allowed to walk around or make contact with innocent pure men!! The infection was fatal!! The prognosis was poor!!

I know what you are thinking; and I don't want to hear it.

"We practically moulded into one organism. Separating us became impossible" *He sighed. Then he chuckled* "One day, she had me tied to the bed and was working on me for the fourth time in succession. It was the 'shout and it gets worse' play. I had already lost the bet and there was premonition in my mind that my heart would not be able to handle this next bout. Safe words were obviously futile. I heard myself say in a quavering voice:

'You know there be no gain to my dying today'

Those sweet intense eyes looked up at me. My pleading face must have looked funny because she suddenly burst into fits of laughter, slithered over my sweating skin and kissed me long and deep, then relaxed on my body.

'You make me very happy, David. Very happy' she said, chuckled throatily, sighed and slept off. I lay there staring at her luscious hair sprayed over my chest. My heart was warm; thankful I had survived but warm. I must have slept off, my hands still tied to the bed frames, because I woke up feeling the throes of pleasure sweeping through me. She was straddling me and doing things I intend not to give picture to. I heard her whimper, shiver and flop on me. Then a voice I didn't know was mine squirmed, and all became quiet. When she came to, she untied my arms and they flopped by my sides lifelessly. She crawled into me and rested.

'What can I do for you?' I asked. I just wanted to be good to her the rest of my life.

'What do you mean? You have been very good to me' She said

'No. All these have been about me. What can I do for you? What are your dreams and fantasies? Do you want to fly private jets? Be a movie star? Shop in Italy? ...' I heard her chuckle. 'No; I am very serious' I raised her face up to me so we can look into each other's face.

She smiled 'I don't have any big fantasies. My fantasy, my dream is something most women will look at and say "you're pathetic". But it's my dream; something I have always cherished and longed for but has always eluded me'

'What is it?'

She thought for a brief minute 'I have always dreamed of being a good man's wife. And you have made me feel like one these past few days. I'm content'

I stared at her. I could not believe my ears. Enigma's only fantasy was to be some lucky bloke's wife! Wow!

'It's impossible to imagine that someone so perfectly hewn is single. How's that?'

'My choice. Relationships can be very complicated. Besides, it's not appropriate now'

'How do you mean?' I asked

'My kind of job; I figure it will be unfair to put someone through the trauma until I retire'

'What job is that?' It was hard to imagine we've not had this conversation for a week now. I knew nothing about this girl and she had been living with me for six days. I don't know how she did that.

She thought about it for a while staring into my face, then she sighed

'I'm a soldier. Special Forces' then quietly 'we go where others cannot go'.

I stared at her. That explained the first night!

Forget first night. That explains a lot of things!

'As a matter of fact, I just came back from an assignment. This is my sabbatical. Relationships cannot be founded on that. So I can only dream. You've made that dream come true' she smiled.

I stared at her in admiration.

'Wow. I watch you guys on TV. Have you ever been hurt?'

She nodded. 'Three times. Last one, I nearly died. Lost behind enemy lines alone. But I survived' She gave a shuddering sigh and cleared her throat.

I could see this was not a discussion she was enjoying. The first time I had noticed her a bit troubled. Who wouldn't be? These people were super humans. I was looking into the face of someone who puts herself on the line everyday so I can live freely. A true hero. I was in awe. There was deep respect for this lady. I felt inadequate beside her and that was saying a lot. And all she wanted was to be treated like a wife. Wow! What a specimen of perfection!

'Come here' I said and she coiled into me and stayed there through the night.

Yep! She was pathetic!

X

The phone woke me the next morning. It was Florence. I needed to get to work. Somethings I needed to do in person. I left Enigma in bed and went to the office. I signed some papers, analysed some issues and coded some web designs and was heading for the door when my office landline started ringing. I left it for Florence to deal with and continued through the door heading past her desk when she signalled for my attention. I looked at her and she mouthed "Mike". I nodded and walked over.

'I just caught him sir. I will put you through' Florence was saying

I took the phone from her. 'Grease man what's up?'

'Finally! Where have you been? Everyone has been looking for you. You don't answer your mobile, you don't return calls; even your secretary could not tell us anything'

I smiled in contentment 'Sorry mate. The story took an entirely different turn'

'What are you on about?' Mike asked

'Do you remember the lady from the party?'

'The Amazon?'

'Yeah; that one'

'I remember you checking her out. Things happened?'

'Yeah'

'Things happened?!! Wow! How was she?'

'The best ever. Literally'

'Wow! Coming from you, that's something! Where did you take her?'

I was reluctant to tell him but he was one of my best friends and I trusted him more than life. 'About that, I ..... I .... I took her home Mike. See, it just happened. There was no time to think –'

'Wait a minute' He interrupted me.

I sighed because I knew what he was about to say.

'Wait a minute' He repeated. 'You took her home?'

I sighed again. 'She's been staying with me now for a week, Mike'

'What?' Mike sounded incredulous. 'What are you doing?'

'I don't know' I sincerely said. 'But this is the first time I have felt content; fulfilled; happy. I can't explain it Mike....' Then I realised it and froze. You see, as I spoke, I realised something that had never happened before with any of the other girls: I had spent a whole week with one girl and no one else had filtered into my mind. Not for once. Thoughts of her made me feel light and bright. Thoughts of her filled my every day even when we or she was doing something else or I was left alone to do my work. She always managed to filter into everything I was doing. The realization hit me like a punch in the gut. My heart started racing. I had found the one. I had found the one! I had found the girl that fits into my fabric with an awesome completeness and she had no fault! This was a miracle! This does not happen. I was riding on a cloud!

'Explain what?' Mike's voice cut into my thoughts.

'Oh my God' I said and started for the door.

'What is it?' Mike asked

'This is it. This is the one' I was talking more to myself now as I drifted in joy

'What are you talking about? You are not making any sense' Mike quipped

'I gotta go Mike. I need to do something' I said as I got to the door.

'Hold it, David!!' Mike snarled. 'What in the world are you talking about?'

'I love her, Mike. I'm in love with her. I gotta go tell her'

'DAVID!!' Mike snarled. That brought me short.

'You didn't have to yell, Mike'

'Don't give me that. What about the others?'

'Don't you see? I have met the one lady that fits into everything I want. I'm gonna have to cut everyone else loose'.

I expected a response but silence greeted me.

'Mike? Mike? Mike!'

'I'm here' He replied,

Silence again. I didn't like that at all. If the strategist among us was lost for words, that meant trouble.

'Say something' I implored

'What do you want me to say?'

I stared into the distance desperately 'I don't know. Something. Anything'

I heard him swallow.

'Are you sure that's wise?' He finally asked

'What else can I do?'

'Good question'

'You should be happy for me'

'Of course I am' He said. He sounded distant. I could perceive he was thinking. 'Do the guys know about this?'

'You're the first'

Another silence

'I'm gonna have to tell them, you know' He finally said

'Yeah, I know'

'We have to discuss this'

I sighed. 'Where are we meeting?'

'We will come to you'

'Okay. Seven?'

'Seven' and he cut the line.

I brooded briefly wondering what line our discussion will tow, tossing up probabilities and weighing out pros and cons.

'What's the problem Sir?' Florence's voice broke into my thoughts. I had briefly forgotten she was there.

I sighed 'My private life is getting a bit complicated'

'A bit?' she chuckled. She could talk to her boss like that. We understood each other so well; it was as if we were siblings.

'A bit more than I'm used to' I said 'It's getting serious. I might be hurting some people very soon'

'I warned you'

'Yeah'

'Want to talk about it?' Florence proposed

'I will give you the outcome, okay' I chuckled mirthlessly and walked off.

XI

The guys arrived at my home as agreed. Enigma and I were in each other's arms just chatting quietly. I don't even remember what we were talking about that night but she uncoiled from me, kissed me and headed for the kitchen

'I'll leave you guys alone' she had said

I went to the door as they banged on the door.

"Banged?"

"We're best of friends. My house was theirs as well. We're that close

I went and opened the door. Sani was in front as usual. I put forth my hand for a handshake. He smacked it away and walked into the middle of the room, Brill and Ken followed, then Mike.

'I wanna see this girl' Sani snarled and turned to face me

'C'mon guys. I thought we were going to be civil about this' I pleaded

'I want to meet the girl!' He emphasized

'I wanna know who this person is, throwing spanners in our works!' Ken said.

'Does she know you have a girlfriend?!' Brill threw in a bit too loudly

Both Mike and I winced at that

'That's not what I expected us to do guys' Mike said 'C'mon'

'Hi' the sonorous voice filtered into the room. Everyone turned towards the kitchen. She was standing by the door, so elegant in her tie-front shirt and shorts, exposing those lovely legs. She had a pleasant smile. 'Nice to meet you'

She brought her hand for a handshake.

Sani's eyes narrowed. 'I know you'

'About that, I am really sorry. Clean slate. Nice to meet you' She repeated, her hand still outstretched towards Sani

Sani ignored the hand and glanced at me, his own eyes conveying 'you stupid, stupid oaf'. But he muttered 'I don't believe this' and walked out of the house.

Enigma gave a wry smile and looked at the others.

I was helpless. I ran after Sani. The others ignored Enigma's still outstretched hand and strolled after us to the outside.

I caught up with him as he got to the car they arrived in. 'C'mon mate. A little bit of respect'

'Respect?!' He snarled 'For who?'

I was dumbfounded.

'Did you give me any respect?!' He continued. 'That was the same girl that insulted me. And you took her home?'

'She was just doing her job. She didn't know who you were' I tried

'Are you defending her now? Against me?' Sani sounded shocked. I was lost for words. 'Well then …' and he entered into the car.

'What's this about, man?' I leaned into the car desperately

He gave a mirthless chuckle. 'Has Pauline come to the house?' He stared into my face. 'Okay, you want to be civil? Let us be civil. What did you expect me to say? How did you expect me to act? I introduced you to Pauline. She has very high respect for me. She trusted me when I told her you were the real deal. She gave herself to you believing you were the real deal. You have been with her for more than a year, close to two. You only gave her the respect of the love Nest. You brought this one home. And you want me to give you respect? Shake your hand and say what's up?' Then he raised his voice to the rest standing behind me 'Can someone take me away from here please!!'

The others came skittering.

'Sorry Mate' Mike said as he entered the car

'Sorry?' Brill snarled 'You messed up big time David. This is not the type you make amends or joke about. That girl will never be accepted in our circles. You know that. So what are you doing?' I tried to speak and he shouted me down 'Dude! You invited her to your home! And from what Mike tells me, you want to cut the rest loose? Because of her?! Man; your stupidity is crossing boundaries. How did you think this was going to play out? Tell me'

Ken was the driver. He walked past Brill towards the wheel as both gave me a stare a mamba would have envied.

'It's your choice mate' He said. 'Your choice' and he climbed behind the wheel and they drove off. I stared after them paralyzed in shock at the turn of events. I had not expected this at all. Yeah, they're vain. Yeah, they're fascist. But c'mon. I'm their friend. I thought they would make an exception. Boy was I wrong.

I gave a shuddering sigh and turned around and headed back to my house. Enigma was standing in the middle of the living room staring into my face, her gorgeous eyes glazed and curious. She looked concerned for me but also had a touch of 'I told you so'. I stalled and we stared at each other. Then she sighed

'Do you want me to go?' She asked

I wondered where that came from.

'What? Why would you ask me that?'

'Your world is shaking because of me. You could potentially lose everything. I would ask you again: Are you sure about this?'

'I'm not sure of anything anymore. All I know is that you make me very happy. And I have fallen in love with you'.

That hit her like a punch. She was not expecting it. Her head literally went back a fraction and her eyes seemed to melt and the radiant child-like beauty took over again

'What could you possibly see here to fall in love with?' She asked in an innocent voice

I sighed and said in my head "You have no idea". I headed for the stairs and as I crossed her, she grabbed my arm gently. I stalled and looked at her.

She searched my face with those intense eyes

'What are you thinking? Tell me. Please; Please'

'I don't know. I'm scared. I can't lose you' I said 'But I'm scared of making a mistake. I'm scared of doing something I will regret forever. I don't know. I look at my options and I break out in a cold sweat. I don't know' I sighed again and headed on up the stairs. She stood there in the middle of the living room deep in her thoughts.

XII

I tossed about through the night unable to sleep. Enigma might have read the mood as she usually does and decided to let me be. I could hear the drone of the TV downstairs. She was giving me space. Wow! This lady should organize a seminar for women on how to handle a man.

Oh, shut up!

Around 3a.m. I couldn't take it any longer. I decided to go down to the kitchen and have a drink to calm my frayed nerves. She was asleep in the living room with the TV still on. I stalled and stared at her lovely figure for a brief while. The thought of her still made me smile even if that evening, it was not as mirthful as I would have wanted it to be. I sighed, gently took the TV remote control from her hand and switched off the TV. Then I went and poured a glass of wine and sat in the kitchen brooding. I had not taken three sips when I heard her coming. I looked up at her. Her face looked tired and drawn. She was unhappy. That alarmed me. I made to stand up. 'Are you alright?'

'I should be asking you' She said tiredly, coming up to me. 'I am so sorry for all the pain I have caused'

'Oh no. Please erase that from your mind. This is not your fault. Not in the least'. I gathered her in my arms as she sat on my lap. She was warm. 'You are the only thing that gives me joy' I said and she gave a slight gasp and hugged me tight crushing her body into me. I reciprocated and felt her whimper and shudder. I sighed contentedly resting my head on her...

XIII

I kissed my girl and made ready to leave for work next morning when my mobile rang. It was Mike.

'Hey?'

'Come down to Sani's house' He said

'Why would I want to do that?'

'Sani's dead'

That did not compute. I stared blankly into space.

'David, did you hear me?!'

'What?' It still did not compute

'I said Sani is Dead' He repeated

'What do you mean?' I managed to babble

'Exactly what I said. He was found by his cleaner this morning. Everyone is over there including the police. I'm on my way!'

I was panting. 'What happened?'

'That's what we want to find out'

I gathered myself together. 'Okay. I will see you there' And we cut the line

'What's the problem?' My girl asked

I turned to her. 'My friend, Sani. He's just been found dead in his home'

She looked at me surprised

'Exactly' I completed

'The one that came here yesterday?' She was concerned

I nodded 'The one from yesterday'

'What happened?' She asked.

'I don't know. I'm off to his house now'

'Alright. Be careful okay' She said.

I gave a sad reassuring smile and headed off.

∘ *   *   *   *   *   *   *₊

Sure enough Sani's house was bustling with activity when I arrived. Police was everywhere. The place was cordoned off with tape. There was quite a big crowd including the Press and the paparazzi. I managed to find my friends.

'Hey' I greeted. 'What's the latest?'

Nobody knew anything yet. The investigation was very much active. While we stood around listening to every word that flew by and ignoring the imploration by the Press to get an interview, I noticed detectives Alfred and Clara step out of the house, under the police tape and head for their car. They were the ones in charge of the case.

'I know those policemen' I said. 'Excuse me'. I hurried over to them. 'Detectives'

'Hey; Mr Reynolds. What are you doing here?' Alfred asked

'Mr Rasheed was my friend. I was with him just last night'

'Last night?' Alfred asked

'Yeah. They came to my house. We had a bit of an argument and they left. I am shocked at this'

Clara's illuminate green eyes studied my face the moment I said that.

'Who is "they"?' Alfred calmly asked

I looked at him surprised. 'My friends. Everyone in London knows my clique of friends'

'Not everyone' Clara said quietly and glanced beyond me into the crowd for a brief while. 'But I see them'.

I was beginning to like this Clara girl. She just seemed not to give a toss!

Clara signalled a uniformed policeman over and muttered something to him and pointed at the crowd. I frowned in anticipation. Something just happened!

'What's going on?' I inquired

Alfred looked at me blandly. 'We would like you to come to the station. All of you'

I reared back 'Why?'

'Part of the investigations. Anything you can help us with. We want to know what happened here last night' Alfred said 'We think you might be able to help us. Is that a problem?'

'I wasn't here last night. He came to my house'

'Still. We would like the details of that discussion. At the station. Will that be a problem?'

I thought about it briefly and shrugged. 'No'

'I didn't think so' Alfred said blandly. 'See you at the station' and he smiled and drove off. I caught a glimpse of Clara's illuminate eyes give me a last glance before the car turned the corner. As I headed to my car, I saw the policeman talking to my three friends ...

*   *   *   *

At the police station, while we waited to be interviewed, I did not fail to notice the tension in the air. Something had happened to our friendship. A chord had been broken. Whatever amendments that could have been made had been totally undone by Sani's death. Somehow I felt they thought it was my fault. Only Mike was talking to me. The rest seemed not to have anything to say to me. My questions met either an awkward silence that Mike tried to dilute even when the questions were not directed towards him; or a monosyllabic answer. At some point, I couldn't take it anymore. I blew up, jumping to my feet:

'What is this? Why is everyone being cold to me? I choose who I want to be with. Not you. Not anybody else'

The three looked at one another, their set faces full of questions

'Don't look at yourselves like that' I roared in disgust. 'You know what I am talking about'

'What are you talking about?' Ken asked coldly

'A friend just died. We are mourning. Or aren't you?' Brill added

'Brill...' Mike cautioned

'Maybe we aren't in the mood to talk'. Ken said. 'Not everything is about you. Once in a while, can we take some time out and mourn a good friend? Or maybe you are not one for mourning friends'

'Or you are too stupid to notice' Brill Concluded

'I'm too stupid to notice?' I asked 'You are the one too imprudent to notice the atmosphere you've created. So stop using Sani as an excuse. Your coldness is because of the girl and nothing else. So let's iron it out here and now'

'David -' Mike tried to calm me down

'If I chose Pauline, you would still need to explain to Deidre why it wasn't her' I said, pointing at Ken 'or Tanya why it wasn't her' Pointing at Brill. 'Sandra, Mike? Everyone seems to forget it's my life. I know what or who makes me happy. Not you. Me'

'Nobody is thinking about your girl, David' Mike said

'This guy irritates me, man' Ken muttered to Brill

'Why don't you say that to my face' I challenged

Ken made to raise his voice

'Ken ...' Mike called out sternly to him.

He gave a mirthless chuckle and looked away

'No. Enough of the peace talks. I want to know what you want to say. Say it to my face. Don't be bickering in the shadows. Come and talk to me' I quipped

Brill jumped to his feet to meet me eyeball to eyeball. The dude was not afraid of anyone. I actually jumped back in surprise 'You know what I hear? I hear conscience talking'

'What?' I asked

'Same here' Ken said his eyes granite. 'There is no going back from this. You're the reason Sani's dead'

Mike sighed 'Ken...'

I stared at him, my initial suspicions confirmed. 'Excuse me?!'

Brill poked me in the chest, his face pugnacious. 'You heard the man'

'Ken; that was uncalled for' Mike snapped

'Hold, hold, hold, Mike' I said, 'What did you say to me?!'

'I knew that guy seven years before I knew you. We go back a long way' Brill said

'We go back a long a way. You come into the pack with stupid penis-oriented decisions and all hell breaks loose!' Ken completed

'Who knows what you said to the police; now, we are here. What stupidity did you display to bring us here?' Brill asked 'Do you ever use your head?'

I only heard one thing in all that accusation.

'Penis-oriented? You two are deluded' I hissed. 'Are you saying because I'm with this girl, that's why Sani is dead?'

'You are just a fool!!!!' Brill roared

And the three of us exploded into unbridled seething argument, talking into one another's faces.

'Guys; guys; Guys!!' Mike hissed fiercely. We all turned to him. 'You are making a scene'

We all turned and down the corridor, Alfred and Clara were staring at us.

'Mr Reynolds, we would see you now' Alfred called.

I looked at my friends 'I can't believe you said that to me. I will remember it'

Ken and Brill swore at me.

I turned to the detectives, gave my friends another glance and nodded soulfully. Their eyes were cold. They were angry. They felt I had broken a sacred cord and there was no mending it again as one of the knots had been burned. As I walked towards the detectives, I knew things would never be the same again.

They showed me into a place like a conference room with a long table and many chairs. It was well lit. They sat together across from me. Alfred's face was friendly although his eyes were intent – cops eyes. The man couldn't help it. Came with the job. His partner was different. Her face was stern but she had her eyes on a file she had come in with, never for once looked up at me. She seemed lost in thought or harnessing information. I don't know.

'What was that all about?' Alfred asked

I sighed it away. 'Family stress'

'You all close?'

I had to think about it. Were we? Would friends turn on their brother like that?

"If you were in their shoes, what would you have done?"

"I would have tried to reason and understand the motive behind the decision. I expected that much. But they just didn't care. They

69

were just blinded with condescending pride over this lady who they obviously felt was beneath their class and blinded by anger because she was in my life. I didn't get it"

'I thought we were' I said to Alfred

'Does this have anything to do with Mr Rasheed's death?'

'Yes. They blame me for it'

'Why?'

I was reluctant. I found it difficult to start discussing my private life with cops, you know. 'It's personal. Very personal'

'Would it have any bearing on our investigation?'

'I doubt it'

'We'll be the judge of that. Tell us about it' came the quiet husky voice beside Alfred. She didn't even look up. Alfred looked at her in surprise.

'I said it was personal' I countered

'Tell us anyway' she said. Then she looked up into my eyes. Boy! That look could melt an iceberg. Those illuminate green eyes had the most disconcerting effect and she knew how to use them. Without saying another word, she conveyed the message poignantly that I better start telling them all they needed to know now or there is a very high chance I might regret it later when I'm charged with withholding information and nobody is interested in listening to what I had to say anymore. She was not going to ask again.

I became concerned 'Hey; I had nothing to do with this'

The seething stare remained.

I sighed

'Ok. Where do I start?' I asked before going on to give them a brief history of my romantic biography. I told them how my life had become a dull bore of routines that I started indulging my fantasies instead of going crazy. How I came across my true-to-life fantasy girl that I thought did not exist but low and behold she did. How she had met every standard I wanted in a woman to the last "T" that I could not believe I was that lucky. How I had wanted to just pack everything in and settle with this girl but my friends had become upset because she was not from our ilk of the society; and how they had walked out on me on our last visit. Next thing I heard Sani was dead.

Alfred seemed confused 'I must have missed something. Did Sani want you for himself?'

'Wow, wow, wow! What kind of question's that?' I exploded

'I'm trying to understand your story' Alfred said

'And of everything I said, that was all you got?'

'The preliminary results say he was under alcohol influence. Forensics initial report says he slipped and banged his head. Do you see where I am going with this?'

'No!'

Alfred smiled. 'That will be all, Mr Reynolds. Thank you'

I stood up to leave.

'What was it about this new girl the rest didn't have?' the husky voice grated across the room

I stalled and turned towards her. Alfred also looked at her puzzled. She was still gazing at her file.

'What do you mean?' I asked

She shrugged her eyebrows 'You wanted to pack it in with this one. What was different about her the others didn't have?'

'What others?' I wanted to know her bases for this line of questioning

She gave a mirthless smile. 'Pauline, Deidre, Sandra, Tanya' Then her illuminate green eyes came up from the file and focused on my face. She must have read my topsy-turvy mind 'You were talking about them on the corridor'

Wow! That was a detective!! She collated the salient points just like that! From a random outburst and argument. I didn't even remember I had mentioned names. Alfred didn't pick the names!

I was reluctant. 'Like I said before, she was a fantasy come true'

'What fantasy is that?' her voice sounded bored and stern but I didn't fail to notice Alfred give her a glance I felt meant "what line of questioning is this?" It did not bother her. She kept her bored gaze on me.

I sighed. 'I have met all niches of girls: the ambitious, the cantankerous, the gentle, the sweet; the emotionally strong that drives a company and it succeeds. There was always something amiss. The ambitious ended up cold, selfish and uninteresting. The cantankerous was no fun to be with. She would give you a high blood pressure. The emotionally strong was full of women liberations and girl-power. It was tasteless. The gentle and sweet sometimes ended up being too soft, needy or boring. You ran a risk of taking her for granted. I wanted more. I started fantasizing about a woman who had all these attributes and none of the weaknesses: was physically very strong and brave yet gentle and sweet, confident in herself but humble about it; strong-character and yet very emotional; absolutely intelligent and yet thoughtful, caring and kind; absolutely upright with morals and yet sensual and wild behind closed doors. And with all these, was very pleasant to look at, you will think she was made out of candyfloss -'

Alfred chuckled 'There's no one like that, mate'

I looked at him 'Come to my house' and I gently headed for the door. When I turned the handle, I looked back at her. Her gaze was still on me, a thoughtful look on her face.

'How did she take the aggression from your friends?' She asked

I shrugged 'Didn't bother her. She was more interested in how I felt. Nothing more'

She nodded, sighed and went back to her file like I was never there. I observed her a while, then looked at Alfred who shrugged so I turned and left the room.

I don't know where the others were but they were not on the corridor when I came out.

I didn't wait for them. I went to work and then went home.

XIV

I didn't hear from any of my friends for a while. As a matter of fact, life rearranged to being without them. I was completely fulfilled going to work and coming back two hours early just to spend time with my woman. After a week, the police informed me that the file had been closed. Sani had died of alcohol-related accident. Although our last meeting was a poor one, he was still one of my very best friends and I missed him dearly. That was my only dim day. I mourned for him. My girl gave me space throughout this time. How she understands a man's needs, I will never know. It's like she reads your mind and knows exactly what you would need. She turned my house into a home. She did shopping; sometimes before I came in and prepared these delicacies you only see in high paying restaurants, sat across from me while we ate and chatted about nonsense and laughed heartily. This was her fantasy and I was willing to play it to her full satisfaction, including the fore-head peck in the morning before I left for work. She loved that one most especially. Always made her smile contentedly, yawn and stretch. I loved seeing that.

Sometimes we play fought. She would let me win even sometimes wincing that I am hurting her, begging me to be gentle. I once made her cry because I pushed her and she slipped and fell on her backside. I consoled her most earnestly. Of course that led to some serious apology lovemaking. Other times, she would again exhibit her immense strength by physically overpowering me and pinning me to the bed. She would show me some of her fighting skills by using some simple moves that completely floored me and she would trap me with her legs in such a way that the more I struggled, the more energy I exhausted. When I was totally spent, she would, in her fluid flexibility, manoeuvre her body over and have her way with me.

Sometimes we played with food or she got right out naughty. Once we were eating and she said I should look under the table. I curiously did and she had her legs –

"I get the picture. Skip that part"

For goodness sake. The graphic pictures were now irksome.

He snorted "She was awesome. Once I was eating this lovely Cantonese lunch she had prepared and I felt her under the table. I didn't even know when she went there. Sent my heart racing, I had a headache. Do you know what she did?"

"I'm not even going there. So, was that the story with Sani then? He had something for you?"

"I'm not even going to dignify that with a response. Safe to say he was not the first. But the closure of the case made Mike call me out of the blue and ask if I was going for the memorial service as the body had already been buried according to Sani's customs. Of course I was. I told my girl about it and asked her if she would come with me

'Are you crazy?' She asked in that her calm sonorous voice

"yeah; are you crazy?!"

"I was so into her, I wanted her everywhere with me. That was the depth of my respect and love"

"You just wanted to showcase her. That was wrong"

"Maybe. I was not thinking at the time. Besides anyone in my shoes will do the same. She was the perfect companion any man could want"

"Why? Because she was soft and answered to your every whim and fantasy"

"No. Because she understood me and was willing to allow me to understand her. And yes, she was humble and answered to my whims. Do you think that made her less of a woman? That's where women get it all wrong. You don't put every man in a box. Men are individually different. Understanding your man's character will tell you how to behave towards him to bring out the best in him"

"Vice versa" I contended

"Precisely. That's why I said she knew me and let me know her. There was no stupid gender generalization with her. Enigma took time and understood me and how to bring out the best in me. Not by being nasty and trying to make me conform. You call it obeying my every whim? Since you have been listening to me, did you by any chance detect any sign of disrespect in my voice for this lady?"

I couldn't argue with that

"And you think she was soft? I watched this lady train and exercise. She was like a machine. She had strength; she had stamina; she had such speed it was heart-stopping. Her flexibility was out of this world"

"I meant emotionally"

"Have you been listening to my story? She was not bedazzled by me. She was in control of herself all the time. She chose to let her inner woman flow towards me of her own accord. Not under duress. That was a very strong woman"

Alright granted I was jealous of this lady. I was looking for excuses. So what?!

"Anyway, back to my story. Maybe it was the news of Sani's immemorial; I don't know. But I was not entirely in a good place that day.

'Why not?' I asked her 'I want everyone to see me with you. We might as well make it official'

She chuckled. 'That's just showing disrespect to your friends. Are you sure you want that heat?'

'I do. How about you?'

She was cleaning a table when I said that. Her eyes came up to my face and she cocked her head to one side wondering what I was on about.

'We've never been seen together outside. Why is that? Are you not proud of me? Don't you want to be seen with me?'

'You are in a bad mood, David. Calm down and take a deep breath. Do not say something you will regret' She said

'Regret? Are you going to beat me up?'

She was taken aback. 'Beat you up? Why would you say that? What are you talking about?'

'No. I want to know: why don't you want to be seen anywhere with me? Why are we still being secretive? I don't get it. I have declared my love for you. I want to make it official…'

'David …'

'No; I don't get it. Is this some on the go fling for you? When you are done, you walk on and leave no trails?'

'David …'

'Don't you care about me enough to make it official? Are you not proud of me? Tell me!'

I didn't understand. Every other girl would jump at the offer to be seen in the social elite. But my girl didn't even like going out much. Nothing of the razzmatazz moved her. She was always calm and in control. As amazing as that was, I felt belittled. Like I had nothing to offer; nothing to bring to the relationship. I was not comfortable with that. But then I had forgotten I was not dating just any other girl but enigma. She didn't jump or raise her voice. She just stared at me. Her face was expressionless but her eyes were steely. It was most unnerving. Then she spoke

'My leave finished two weeks ago. I'm currently on AWOL. The American government is looking for me. When they find me, which they will, I will go to jail. I will be dishonourably discharged. I will lose my pension. All I have ever worked for has gone down the drain. Why do you think I possibly did that?'

I stared at her speechless. She gave a mirthless lop-sided smirk and walked off towards the kitchen. I went after her.

'Why would you do that?' I gasped

'Now you ask'. She started cleaning the work surface. Her face was set. I came up beside her and placed my hands on her wrists. She sighed and looked up at me, her eyes glazed.

'I'm sorry. I really am. I was not thinking. I am so excited about you; I want the whole world to know. You see, I feel so inadequate beside you. I want to know you care about me as much as I care about you. I want to know we are taking this plunge together; as much as it scares me …' I sighed. 'I guess I was only thinking of me. I never thought of how you feel. Your own sacrifices. I will never do that again. I am so sorry'

We stared at each other. She smiled and came close. We kissed passionately and crumbled to the floor.

Later, we lay in each other's arms, each lost in their thoughts. After what seemed a long time, I sighed. 'I can't believe you did this'

'You wanted a relationship. I told you I couldn't do relationships while doing my job. I can't do my job if my mind is distracted. I had to choose'. She rolled over on her back so she could look into my face. 'I have fallen in love with you David. That has never happened before.' She sighed deeply 'Now I am scared. I have something to lose. That is not healthy for the kind of job I do. You don't do my kind of job with fear in your heart. You will die in your first mission. I do not intend to die'

'I'm not worthy of you. No man is'

She looked into my eyes 'You are'

I couldn't believe a woman like this would fall for me so deeply.

So deeply.

'But your job makes you happy' I tried

She gave her innocent childlike smile 'You make me happy'

At that moment, I decided to propose. This was the woman for me. This was the woman I was going to spend the rest of my life with. 'Can I ask you something?'

She jumped to her feet and started dressing up.

'What's wrong?' I was confused

'There's someone at the door. You don't want her to see you like this before a fight'

'Her?'

'Start dressing up' She urged but her innocent eyes were soft on me. She was already in her shorts and putting on her T-shirt

'Nobody comes to the house unless invited. Besides, I didn't hear anything' I said. I didn't like the moment being ruined like this

'You will' and she was out of the kitchen heading for the stairs.

I sat there wondering what just happened. Sure enough there was a thumping on the door and a female voice bawled out my name. I jumped to my feet and started dressing up, my mind racing. I knew who was at the door. Who gave her my actual address? Then how did Enigma know two minutes before it happened that there was someone at the door? That it was a girl? And that there would be a fight?! Was it her perfume again? I didn't perceive anything! 'DAVID!! Open the damn door!! I know you are in there!!'

I hastily rounded up dressing and hopped towards the door as fast as I could. I had respectable neighbours who didn't like noise at all. I swung the door open knowing apprehensively what was about to go down but hoping I would handle it well.

Deidre pushed past me and stormed into the house. 'Where is she?'

I didn't know how to answer that. I stared at her, my mouth open. She headed for the stairs. I circled round her to block her path from going any further and attempt to contain any arising situation in the living room

'You can't deny it. I know the whole truth. I can't believe you did this to me! Me! I gave you everything I am. Where is she?!'

And she pushed through me and stormed on. I ran after her trying to explain.

'Deidre; it has nothing to do with her. It was all me. I know you're going to hate me for this. And I am truly sorry. I don't know what else to say'

'I already hate you' she said panting heavily as she went from room to room. She was obviously primed for war and she could smell blood.

My heart was thumping. I didn't know what to expect

'Where is she?! I want to see her!'

As every room we checked was empty, I was growing confident that Enigma had hidden herself effectively.

'No. Please. No. It is for the best' I said

She stalled at some point and turned to me 'So this is it. You penis-oriented rabbit!'

Penis-oriented?! Yeah. I knew who told her where to find me.

'You did this to me?' She continued 'You did this; to me. All they said about you were true, weren't they?'

'All who said?'

She looked past me. Enigma had suddenly appeared from one of the guest rooms she had been in. I guess she wanted to peek not knowing that Deidre was looking in that direction.

'YOU!!!' Deidre roared and rushed at her. I called after her desperately as Enigma raised her arms apologetically in surrender. It was obvious she had not meant to cause this lady any pain. But Deidre was blinded with rage. She piled into Enigma with such force, I winced.

Deidre reeled backwards and sprawled while Enigma stood her ground quite still, looking at her through sad eyes. I don't know what she did but it seemed to reverse the impact of the force on the person that executed the force. I did not understand it but the impact was mind numbing. I could not believe it. I stared in astonishment. Deidre stared in horror, the breath knocked out of her. She whimpered, coughing as she gathered herself together. I ran to her

'Are you alright?' I asked earnestly.

Deidre did not answer me. She could not talk. She was panting. She clambered to her feet, still staring at Enigma, her mouth hanging open. Without a single word she headed for the door. At the door, she looked at me. Her eyes were glazed and flat. I had never seen her look like that before. She looked from me to Enigma and back.

'Deidre, let's talk about this. Please' I pleaded

'You will regret this. And you will suffer' She hissed. Then she left my house.

'Deidre ...' I called after her but she ignored me and went into her car and drove off. I sighed and went into the house. Enigma was sitting on the stairs. She gave me a sad smile; sad understanding smile.

How can one be so understanding and accommodating?

'I'm so sorry about that' I said

'It's alright. Now you understand. I can't be seen outside with you. It's for your own good. These are very powerful people and they will try to hurt me to get to you. And I will be forced to protect myself'

'Nobody will dare hurt you' I said brokenly but intensely and I meant it.

She smiled softly. 'Do you think so?'

XV

"Did you have a visit from any of the other girls?"

"Yeah. Very scary experience, I must say.

About a week after the incident with Deidre, on a dull Thursday evening, we had just finished supper and were playing with pillows. I had made a joke and Enigma was laughing heartily when the doorbell rang. She went to answer it while still chatting with me. She had not been primed to anything so I had nothing to worry about. She opened the door still giggling

'So, it's you' came the gentle voice outside

Enigma's giggle petered out and she became quiet. They observed each other

'So, you are the new girl?' Came the gentle voice again.

Then I knew who it was and sprang to my feet and rushed to the door.

'Tanya!' I exclaimed then I couldn't put words together. I thought desperately for a sentence to make and nothing came to me

Both girls stared at each other. Tanya's densely thickset and polished frame was squeezed into this sleeveless leather outfit that made her very intimidating. She wore these tight leather trousers and high boots. Her firm arms and breasts strained against the inner spandex that completed her intimidating presence. She was just an inch shorter than Enigma. Spent most of her free time in the gym keeping fit. Emotionally Tanya was a tad distant and her sexual prowess was rough. I had to wince through it sometimes. I liked her a lot though because she was very intelligent and could match a good intelligent discussion but she never really tugged my heart like Enigma did. Nobody ever did.

That hurts!!

I don't know how she did it but Enigma was soft and hard at the same time. Hot and cold when you wanted her to be; sweet, available, and yet strong. I don't know how to explain it. I'd say she was all encompassing. Like she was my own particular missing rib; if you can say that.

I cannot say that!!

'Would you like to come in?' I finally blurted out

They stared at each other like I was not there. Tanya has always been intimidating but that day, she looked ominous. Her eyes were dim and flat. I was really unnerved. I swallowed hard unsure what was about to happen. To my amazement, Enigma seemed unperturbed but there was a glint of curiosity in her eyes as she looked Tanya over.

'Yeah' She said in that quiet sonority. 'I'm the new girl'

A slight smile flitted across Tanya's lips. 'I was once the new girl'

'Not anymore' Enigma replied after a brief silence.

You could slice the tension with a knife as they looked each other over. Then Tanya gave me a dress-down look that made me feel this small.

'Okay' she said and turned and walked off. 'Let's go'

That's when I saw the three girls in gothic leather high boots and net hosiery outfits sitting on her Mercedes C-class licking lollypops. They all practically had the same face. They all looked at Enigma whose eyes moved from one to the other. They promptly came down from the car hood and entered inside. Tanya joined them. She and Enigma gave each other one last look and the car drove off. Now I knew what Enigma meant by these were very dangerous and powerful people. Suddenly I realised I may not be as powerful as I thought I was. I maybe liked. Even a tad famous but when it came to the down and dirty, I was a complete novice!! To think Enigma knew this shocked me. I suddenly felt so ineffectual and small. There was something I didn't know about my circle of friends! Who were the triplets with Tanya?! I have never seen them before!

'So; where were we?' Enigma's words broke into my thoughts. I looked at her. She was smiling again.

Smiling?!

Smiling!!

'This is not funny' I whined

She shrugged and closed the door, moving away from it. 'You wouldn't let that spoil our mood? I was truly enjoying this evening. I felt so complete and at peace'

Well I didn't!!

'How come this is not bothering you?'

'Why should it?' Enigma was surprised

'I dated Tanya for two years. I have never seen that side of her before. I have never seen the triplets before!'

Enigma chuckled sweetly. 'Now you have. Life goes on'

I kept staring at her desperately.

Enigma sighed. She was not happy that her lovely evening was being ruined by this. But she felt she needed to give me an explanation which obviously I was not aware of. 'That's the thing with matters of the heart. It brings out the good and the bad in all of us, no matter who you are. I knew this was going to happen. They have exposed your secrets to defame you. Now, everyone sees you as a weasel and they are disgusted'

Weasel? I resent that

'But most importantly, they are curious about this girl that changed your mind' She continued. 'Knowing now where you live, they are all coming over to see who I am. First one came with the expected jealous rage. That, I find hard to handle. This one came with intimidation. That's within my arc. I'm very comfortable with it' Then she suddenly broke into this childlike innocent smile that made her look so sweet 'I feel so important. Thanks to you; I have never been this valued in my life'

'They looked so dangerous' I whined

She kept smiling with this relaxed peaceful air around her 'Well, I'm the one they want to hurt' then she winked at me as she snuggled into me happily...

She always managed to make everything bright. It was so reassuring that she was not worried that it almost brought tears to my eyes. I had nothing else to say. I just gathered her in my arms and we started kissing. I'd leave it there.

That's perfectly alright by me

A week or so later, thanks to Enigma, I had completely forgotten about the Tanya incident. Another knock on my door and Enigma went to open it again. They seemed to know days we were in a very good mood, I tell you.

She was still answering to a joke I had made as she opened the door. A slap connected with her cheek. It was distinct and sharp. I flinched at the sound. A second and probably a third slap were intended but none got to their destination because she reacted with the speed I had come to know. She parried the first hand and grabbed the second wrist mid-air. Then I heard a female voice squirm and start yelping. I rushed to the front door. It was Pauline. Sweet tender Pauline coming to show how unhappy she was. I felt sorry for her. She had intended to rain slaps on Enigma but only connected once because Enigma was unprepared and unaware. As Enigma squeezed the wrist, Pauline could not shout anymore. She desperately tried to punch her way out of it but none of the punches were having any effect on Enigma whose deadpan face stared flatly at her. She whimpered and went on her knees, sweat beads appearing on her face.

I saw all these in a second and I rushed Enigma.

'Wow, wow, wow, wow' I cried. 'Don't. Stop please; stop! Please!'

Enigma had a clenched fist ready to plant. But she thought better of it and let Pauline go. Pauline cupped the wrist and started to bawl. I hugged her and started to apologise. Enigma walked back into the house quietly.

Pauline suddenly shrugged me off

'Get your hands off me!!' she snarled and crying, ran to her car and drove away. I stared after her for a while before turning into the house. This time Enigma was not smiling. She was not happy that someone had been physical with her and she was not happy she was not keyed to her environment anymore. She felt she was getting too comfortable and that disturbed her

I sat beside her quietly and after a little while, I took her hand in mine and looked at her.

'I'm sorry' I said

She looked at me, her eyes flat. 'From now on, you open your doors' And she stood up to go upstairs. 'Something is brewing. And I don't like it'

Boy, was she right about that......?

XVI

In the next few weeks, quite insidiously, things started going pear shaped. Suddenly it was as if no one liked me anymore in our circles. My contracts and retainers suddenly felt their businesses were better off elsewhere. Phone calls reduced in frequency. References that my friends provided for me in the past were rescinded. I was maligned from social gatherings. My companies were investigated for things I knew nothing about, almost putting me in disrepute. My luck was the intrinsic intelligence of the detective teams that investigated me. They noticed inconsistencies in their investigations and realised someone was trying to darken my reputation so they let me be and tried to trace their sources of information. Seemed like whoever was doing that realised the same intelligence of the police department and withdrew their pressure. However the damage was done and my clientele waned significantly. Reports from my ship captains became quite uninspiring and discouraging. Three ships had to combine their goods into one once to make a profitable journey. One Ship suddenly sank in the middle of the Mediterranean, costing me more than twenty-six million in assets and compensations. My bank accounts significantly slumped after that. Some of my harbour workers had to be laid off pending improvements. I remember coming to work once and found Florence playing games on YouTube because there was nothing to do. That shocked me. I spent the morning brooding. At some point, I could not take it anymore, I called Ken. He was the one that rescinded his references for me. That cost me quite a packet. He did not take my call. I left a message begging him to rethink. He did not get back to me. I called Brill to ask him to speak to one of my major clienteles he was very close to. He didn't even let me get a word in edgeways. Just exploded on me on how I thought I was the leader of the group and important. How they would show me I was nothing in this town. That I was propped up by them; that everything I had was from them, bla, bla, bla, bla, bla. At some point I kept the phone on speaker and went to do something else and let him drone on. He really gave it to me. By the time he was done, I felt so little. I took a sigh and just said 'I'll speak to you later then'. He swore at me and cut the line. 'Now that's what I call being pissed' I said to myself. I went to put my jacket on and felt something warm down my cheek. I wiped it and realised I was crying! Why was I crying?

"There are tears in your eyes now"

He blinked them away and smiled sadly.

"Yeah. I loved those guys. I still do. I didn't know they didn't like me. At all"

"Well, if you ask me, anyone that tries to destroy your life and career over something as small as this, is not your friend. You my dear have your priorities askew to still love them. There is nothing you have told me so far that warrants what they had done. If someone does not like me, they can go their way, I'd say"

"You know, I thought the same thing. I felt no matter what the problem was, a bit of displeasure, a bit of angry tantrum and swear words and we were content and even. I didn't expect incisive attacks. They almost got me bankrupt over this. They were willing to destroy me permanently over a relationship that had nothing to do with any of them. I didn't get where the aggression was coming from. Was it because Sani died? Was it because of the girls? Were they gaining anything from my dating the girls? Why would Sani get drunk and kill himself because of a perception of disrespect by me? And why would the others buy into it and go all out to deal with me in revenge? I know in my ilk, I admit, we think like children. But c'mon. Not to this extent. It didn't make any sense.

Anyway, I called Mike and asked for his help. He explained to me that doing anything for me obviously would put him in people's bad books so whatever he did would be hidden but he would try all he could. I thanked him and left the office as there was no work to be done.

He never got back to me

'Never say "I told you so"' Florence whispered as I walked by her.

I stalled and looked at her hurt face. I gave her a mirthless reassuring smile. 'It will be sorted'.

I didn't believe it either.

I longed to get home. The arms of my woman were the most relaxing place to be.

Since contracts were not coming up as frequently as they used to, I stopped going to the office. I gave instructions to Florence to follow. I stayed home and enjoyed my woman's company. She had a way of making your problems seem a distance away.

For goodness sake!!!

For three weeks, everything was lull. She kept my spirits up. Kept a smile on my face and kept me believing there was a light at the end of a very dark tunnel. Days that were meant to be a misery were turned into sumptuous sexual adventures. I forgot my business empire was at the brink of collapse. Everyone that met me did not understand why I was still smiling. My heart was very hopeful that things will definitely turn around...

Then one evening, things started to happen. I had gone to a mall and bumped into Mike. It had been a while. He had not got back to me after my phone call. We talked a bit then he asked me if my woman was still around. It came up in the midst of reiteration of some of our in-house jokes but it did not fail to hit me. I looked at him

'She is for keeps, Mike. Never been sure of anything else in my life. She is staying with me. Forever'

He sighed and scratched his forehead 'How can I help you if you keep giving me answers like that'

'What do you mean?' I asked

Mike shrugged. 'A lot of people are going to be very unhappy about this'

'They have already shown me how unhappy they can get'

'Oh no; it can get worse' He said

I stared at him. 'How do you mean?'

He shrugged and chuckled. 'Very powerful people are hurt. You were incommunicado. We had to tell the girls. They told their parents; their friends; people talked. Next thing, anger rose'

I stared at him. I understood the girls. What was it to others? Their friends? My contracts? My retainers? It didn't make sense. It was driving me crazy.

He shrugged again. 'When messages change hands, they metamorphose. Who knows what people have heard about you?'

'What is it to people who I settle with?'

He shrugged and gave a smile. 'Why do people shoot down a politician because he groped a girl? Does that affect his work efficiency? No! Will it affect his ability to represent his people intelligently? No. But the image matters, mate. The image matters. People can make very nasty decisions based on hearsay. That's the world we live in. The Press thrives on that. The world revolves on hearsay. Majority of our lifestyle is based on hearsay. You of all people should know that' He stared intently at me. 'You are not the only shipping company in England. Hearsay made people come to you. Hearsay will make them walk away as well. Remember that'

He had a point. I felt helpless. I sighed and made to go.

'Hey' He said. 'I'm always here for you. I'll wait'

I nodded gratefully.

We talked of a few other things and said our goodbyes.

On my way home, I thought about the events of the months gone by. I remembered Becky's warning and how I had snagged it to shreds feeling I was an important person in this country and would be treated as so. I remembered Enigma asking me every step of the way if I was sure of my decision to be with her.

These girls knew!! They understood the implications and wide ramifications of my decision. They knew my world of people more than I did. They knew just how infinitesimal my so-called power was and yet they respected me, nonetheless.

Gosh, I felt low. I sighed deeply as I started to work out scenarios of how to get back on my feet again. I needed to if I was going to get out of this quagmire.

Enigma; That lady. She knew the heat of my decision to be with her would fall on her and yet she accepted to stay with me. What sort of girl was this?! I didn't deserve her!! Not in the least. I made up my mind. I was going to make this girl happy!! I was bent on it, no matter what. Instead we will migrate to some country somewhere if that will bring us peace but I intended to make this girl happy.

I came back to the house and found it empty. My girl was gone. Her wardrobe was empty. Her bags were missing. I was horrified. My heart started to race. I was panting as I looked around for her. She was nowhere to be found. She had refused to have a mobile phone so I could not call. She always said it made it easier for someone to be tracked. Said since she was not intending to go anywhere, there was no need for one. What paranoia.

There was nowhere to assume she had gone. So I became really nervous and called the police and requested to speak to Alfred.

'My Girlfriend has gone missing'

'Since when?' Alfred asked me

'Since today'

'Well, Mr Reynolds, it's not yet twenty-four hours for you to get –'

I interrupted him there 'Some powerful people have threatened me. I fear they may have done something to her to get to me'

'Why would anybody want to do that?' He seemed to feel I was going paranoid over nothing

'Please come!' I snapped and cut the line. I called Mike but his phone was unreachable. None of the other guys would speak to me so I didn't bother.

Then I realised: I actually did not have anyone apart from those four who were friends I could actually call friends. How did I get so isolated in life without knowing it? I was beside shocked. When did this happen? I used to be the guy with all the friends, both powerful, influential and minion. When was I deserted? What went wrong?

I walked in circles in my home, my trepidation mounting with every passing minute. The wise usually tell you not to hang out with people you won't gain anything from. Well, that's a load of hogwash. I had spent my time building businesses. A lot of crowd that were only business associates. Nobody I could truly call a friend except those four because I felt I was not gaining anything from anybody else; rather people were gaining from me. I had no one to pour my heart to if those four were not around. Well, now they were not around anymore. I guess the wise did not anticipate my life story when they were stating their words of wisdom. The whelps.

Who are we to judge that someone is not important? That someone cannot bring a meaning to your life? Who are we to decide that? What are the standards of measuring who might or might not be important in our lives' journeys?

Soon the police car arrived. Alfred and his partner climbed out. She had on this skin-tight jean trouser and jacket. She had a t-shirt on the inside. She had her hands in her pockets and she walked tersely behind Alfred. She obviously didn't like being in this part of town and she had the same look Alfred had: they felt this was a waste of man hours. But since I was an important part of the police charity, they felt they owed me this. But I also felt this was not something they would want to do very often. I shouldn't expect them to be at my beck and call.

"Hang on! In the heat of the moment, you noticed what she was wearing?"

"No. I just remembered it now as I'm telling you the story. Why are you asking?"

I shrugged. "Just curious"

"About what?"

"Sorry. Please continue"

"I hurried to them.

'She's not yet back' I said

'Calm down, sir. Let's go inside and talk' Alfred said and actually led the way.

I noticed Clara had stopped and was looking around the environment, taking it in.

Really?! She came for sight-seeing?! I asked myself

'Are you coming?' I asked her

She gave me her bored look. 'Yeah, you go ahead' her husky voice said.

'I hope you are taking this seriously' I complained

She studied my face briefly with those illuminate eyes 'Okay, I will lead the way then' and she walked past me and headed for the house. I sighed and ran after her.

Inside, Alfred stood at one corner and asked me to tell him everything. There wasn't much to tell. I had a phone call asking me to get to the office regarding a contract that was taken from me. I went for the meeting. The client's terms were crazy so the discussion fell through. On my way home, I got a call from one of my friends, Mike who told me he was nearby at a shopping mall. I went to see him. Then came straight back home and found her gone including her bags.

'How long did you stay at the office?' Alfred asked

'About an hour and then about an hour at the mall'

'And you don't think she had left of her own accord?'

'No. there was no reason to. She had settled with me. Why? She even admitted to me recently that she loved me'

'Maybe that's why she left' Clara said quietly

I was not expecting that from the husky-voiced one. I was so irritated; it took all in me to keep sane. 'What? That doesn't even make sense'

'And it makes sense that someone came into your house and kidnapped her, no forced entry, did not scatter your house, did not break anything and had time to pack her bags?' Her eyes narrowed to emphasize her point.

She had taken in the whole scene, noted all the points she had just made, percolated them and made her conclusions and I had not seen her touch anything or even noted her eyes move. Despite my anger, I was impressed, to say the least. These people's minds worked like electricity.

'I don't like the way you talk to me' I said sternly to her

I noticed her swallow and look away. She was humbled I had stood up to her!

However I tossed her points around in my mind. They seemed robust. How possible were my suspicions? Was I overreacting in fear? Has she really left me? Has she realised I was not worth the trouble? I wouldn't blame her though; the selfish person that I am? I'd left a long time ago.

But yet, I still felt something was not adding up. Something was amiss. She had given up so much for this relationship to just pack up one morning and leave without me seeing the signs; without us talking about it at least; without her telling me she was leaving.

'Alright Sir; why would you think something has happened to her?' Alfred asked 'Nothing here is pointing in that direction'

'She was very happy here. She was very happy with me. She was going to cook a Taramasalata and briam combination today with a tad of Zucchini salad just to prove to me that Greek diets were more delicious than Chinese'

'A what?' Clara asked

'And we had a dress down bet on it for this evening' I continued. 'That is not the discussion you have when you are planning to leave a person. She would not leave without telling me. That's the thing with her: she wears her heart on her sleeve. She's not pretentious. She says what she means. She is physically very strong; she is not afraid to tell you as it is so why not tell me if she wanted to leave?'

'If she was strong, how were they able to overpower her and kidnap her without a single tell-tale sign in the house?' Alfred asked

'Because they didn't do it here' the sonorous voice came from the door. We all swivelled and Enigma was standing by the door, dishevelled, bruised and dirty. She was bleeding from a cut under the eye and the side of the forehead. We didn't even hear her walk across the courtyard to the building and it was all cobbled stone flooring. We didn't even know she was near until she was standing in our midst.

I rushed and hugged her tight. She winced a bit. I drew back and looked into her face. It was set. Her eyes were flat. She was studying the detectives. I stepped away and looked from her to the detectives. They were studying her too. She seemed tensed up; like an animal that was caged; like she was going to explode. I have never seen her like that. Another peel of the onion sheath revealed.

'What did they do to you?' I cried

'Here; come and sit down' Alfred said. He sounded very caring and made to help.

She nodded her "never mind; I can do it myself" and sat down and took a shuddering sigh. I sat beside her, still looking at her face.

'What happened?' I persisted

'Do you think you can talk? Or do you want us to take you to the hospital and speak with you later' Alfred asked.

She stared from one detective to the other for a brief while, sighed and then nodded. 'I can talk'

'Can you tell us what happened?'

'I was buying groceries. They appeared from nowhere. They had guns'

'Guns?!' I cried shocked

'Hang on, sir' Alfred said with a restraint that felt like he wanted to say "Shut up, dude; I'm trying to listen!!"

She looked at me softly and gave me a weak smile. 'I froze and just followed them. They put a bag over my head and put me in a car. I don't know how long we drove. Then they pushed me out of the car'

'They pushed you out of a moving car?' Alfred asked

She raised her arms. Her sleeves were blood soaked. Her fingers were covered in caked blood. There were strait bruises down her fore arms that looked like results of chafing. The flawless skin was ripped in shreds. I couldn't take it anymore. I gasped and stood up and went to the wall to fight back tears. From the corner of my eye, I noticed the female detective gave me a glance but still concentrated on my girl. It was hard to miss: those illuminate green eyes were like torches. If they moved you noticed it. That girl should be a Watch Tower.

'What happened after they pushed you out?' She asked

Enigma glanced up at her 'How do you mean?'

The detective shrugged 'What happened next?'

'They drove on. Luckily for me, there were no cars coming. I wouldn't be here' Enigma said

I snapped and turned towards her 'They wanted to kill you? Did you see the people that did this?!'

'Sir; Please; calm down. Let us ask the questions' Alfred said 'Please'

His attempt at soothing my pain actually made it worse. I felt my eyes burn with tears so I walked away to the bar and stooped onto it trying to control myself

'Did they say anything to you throughout the whole time?' I heard Clara ask.

There was silence. I turned in curiosity and Enigma was giving me a broken look.

'What did they say?' the husky voice pushed

'Since I didn't want to leave, they would make me leave. I would disappear forever. Everyone would think I packed my things and left. No one will ever know what happened' she said quietly

'That's why they packed your things' Alfred concluded

Clara was staring at Enigma strangely. Her phone started to ring as well as Alfred's. Alfred picked his. Clara ignored hers.

'Why do they want you to leave?' Clara asked 'What is their stake in his relationships?'

Enigma shrugged gently. Then after a pause 'I presume because

I'm not part of their ilk'

'Bit drastic' Clara said

Enigma sighed. 'Tell them that'

'If you see these people again, would you recognize them?' she asked

Enigma looked at her for a brief while 'I had a bag over my head'

'Their voices?' Clara asked again.

Enigma thought for a brief while 'No'

'Okay' Clara said and turned to Alfred.

'We are needed at the office' Alfred said to her. 'Alright. We will leave you two alone now' He said to us.

I panicked. 'What if they come back?'

'We can give you police protection' Alfred offered

'I doubt they will come back' Clara said 'Not with you in the house' I didn't understand what she meant. 'This was supposed to happen without your knowledge. Don't let her out of your sight'. And she moved for the door. 'We'll keep in touch. You are not going anywhere are you?'

Enigma looked at her. They observed each other for a brief second. Enigma shook her head slowly, her eyes looking tired

'No' she quietly said.

'You are sure you don't want us to take you to the hospital?' Clara asked

'I'm sure' Enigma replied

'Those wounds look really bad' Clara concluded

'I know' Enigma concluded

Both ladies stared blandly at each other.

'Don't worry. We will catch the people that did this' Alfred said and left. Clara swept from Enigma to me and back to Enigma with her green lustre. Enigma turned her broken look towards her injuries. Clara stepped outside.

I stared after Clara as she went towards their car. She and Alfred chatted a bit and Alfred abruptly looked in my direction. I frowned.

Clara looked at him and threw her hands in the air in exasperation

'What was that for?' she asked

They entered their car, Clara still chewing Alfred's ear and they drove off.

'Don't worry about it. They are the police. They are paid to be suspicious' Enigma said, her voice with a little shiver. She was trying hard to contain the pain she was in.

I turned to her

'Suspicious? Why on earth would they be suspicious?'

'Because I came back alive. She feels I'm not telling her everything'

'She?'

'Yeah; She. She is the one that does not believe me' She sighed.

'That is ridiculous' I cried.

Enigma stood up and headed for the bathroom. 'Yeah'

XVII

I spent the evening pondering about the whole event, my mind going topsy-turvy. Why would anybody want to kill her?

Kill her?!!

My goodness!! This was out of control.

Kill her!!!

For what?! What is so important about who I date? Who is it important to? The girls? Their parents? Who stands to gain from a relationship with me? No answer that makes sense came to me. None of the girls were from mafia families or even into anything rough. What was this all about? I called Mike again for the eleventh time and still no answer. Something was up and I didn't know what. I couldn't call any of the girls. That was out of the question. I was not that stupid.

I walked around the house, lost in thought, pondering hard and getting more confused as I did so. I heard her in the bathroom down the corridor and I went to her. She was standing under the shower motionless. It was as if she was lost in thought as well. The blood had been washed off her. The injuries were red and raw. I felt sick with pain just looking at them. She seemed oblivious of the pain. I came close. My movement made her twitch and she looked in my direction. For a split second, I saw a flash of the flat eyes again before it disappeared and was replaced by the innocent one. I don't know how she does that but it was scary. One minute she looked as menacing as a mamba about to strike and the next second, she was a childlike sweetness. I guess the soldier and the woman in love were all in the same body. Depends on which one was dominant at any time.

'Hey' I said. 'Can I give you a scrub?'

She smiled and let me into the cubicle. I surveyed the injuries. I couldn't even imagine what she was going through.

'I am so sorry about this' I choked, realising how empty my promises in bravado of protecting her were; and the desolation I felt, knowing she knew all along. There was nothing special about me. I was like everyone else – all air and no substance. How could she know and still love me? I didn't understand it.

She smiled again, touched my chin and lifted up my face to meet her stare. I don't know how my face looked but she seemed touched by my look. She kissed me gently. I sighed and she kissed me again more intently. I enquired with my eyes but without saying a word, she dragged me close and crushed her lips on mine. Right there in the cubicle we had some aggressive sessions that left me totally worn, waned and sore. It was a bit bizarre but lovely. I could hardly walk when we were through. We went and slumped on the bed.

'How are you feeling?' I asked. She smiled and crawled into me and it was not long, she was breathing even. I admired her child-like face, now with fresh bruises and wondered why anyone would want to hurt this individual, so sweet and serene. I was still thinking about it when I dropped off.

We must have been really worn because we slept like logs through the night and morning. I woke mid-afternoon with a jerk. I surveyed my room, realising where I was. Then I saw her lying peacefully by my side. I admired her as she slept, for a brief while before I decided to go downstairs for a drink of water. I put my dressing gown on and strolled downstairs. Everywhere was quiet and serene. I went into the kitchen and poured myself a drink. My mind was still pondering over the events of the day before, trying to figure things out. I shrugged out of my thoughts and sighed. I made to take a sip of water when I was suddenly grabbed in a steely vice grip; a hand clasped my lips shut and the cup of water was professionally taken off my hand without a sound.

'Shhhhh' came a voice behind me. 'Do not struggle sir. It is for your own good'

Then a uniformed policeman appeared in my field of view and quietly asked where my girlfriend was. I pointed upstairs. He looked sideways and nodded. That's when I saw a whole platoon of armed policemen stealthily manoeuvre upstairs like a machine. How they came into my house without my knowing, I cannot tell. I had heard nothing.

'Gently sir, let's head to the living room' The one holding me said. 'No sudden moves, please'

I obeyed and we transferred to the living room and he held me, backing himself against a wall and waited. Some armed policemen were on the staircase, battle-ready while others moved for my bedroom.

I mumbled. The policeman with me looked at me wondering, releasing my lips

'What is going on' I asked.

Two others gestured at me to keep quiet.

The one holding me did not reply. He clasped my mouth again and focused on the operation happening in the moment.

Next I heard my bedroom door crash, orders were barked and all went quiet. I heard her reply gently. The leader of the operation said something. Then all went quiet for a brief while. Then footfalls came down the stairs as Alfred and Clara walked in with their team. They both had plasters on the side of their faces. There was a discolouration and a slight swell on Clara's jaw. Alfred had a red eye. Clara gave me a brief look and turned towards the corridor as the uniformed policemen led Enigma out. She was in T-Shirt and trousers and handcuffed. The wounds on her arms were dressed in neat bandages. I don't remember when that was done. She must have woken up at night to sort them.

As I saw her, I started to mumble loudly. The cop holding me let go of my mouth

'What's going on?! I demand to know what this is all about!!' I shouted. Alfred looked at the cop restraining me and gave a nod. The cop released me completely and stepped back. I glared at him.

'Sorry Sir. Orders' He said apologetically. They all knew me in the police force and the millions I have poured into their charities. He was not happy to manhandle me.

'What is this all about?' I demanded

Clara ignored me and looked into Enigma's eyes. Enigma met her gaze unflinching. They observed each other for a brief while

'What's this about?' Enigma asked quietly, her face bored

'You are under arrest for the deaths of Mr Brill Yates and Mr Ken Stanford ...'

"What?!!"

My reaction exactly.

Enigma's face was expressionless. There wasn't even a hint of surprise, either pretentious or not. I could not comprehend it.

'...and the attempted murder of Mike Staples' Clara finished

I saw surprise come into Enigma's eyes and to my shock she said 'Attempted?' before she realised herself.

Clara seemed to catch that and smiled mirthlessly. 'He didn't die. He can hold his breath for a long time.'

What?!! What in the world was going on?!!! Enigma?! My friends?!! Dead?! Her?!! Them?!! Mike?!! My mind could not take it. I went blank still staring morosely at the scene. To say I was stupefied would be the understatement of the decade.

Everyone around me was talking but their voices sounded hollow to me and reverberatingly hazy. The two women observed each other saying things with their eyes only they understood.

'Take her away' Clara said finally. That was the only distinct sentence I heard there.

I stood speechless as everyone left and Alfred's team went to work searching my house from top to bottom. I was unable to find the words to say. I just stared.

Alfred walked up to me 'We would need you at the station, sir. We would like to know what you know'

I stared at him for a while before understanding he had said something. 'What?'

'We would appreciate it if you could come to the station' Alfred said. I kept staring at him. 'I will wait for you'

That was supposed to prod me but I was still staring in shock. My heart was paralyzed. I couldn't think. My mind was blank.

I would be!! My goodness!!

'Sir?' Alfred enquired.

My stomach churned and I tossed everything on the rug. Alfred rushed me to the nearest bathroom where I wretched a few more times and then collapsed on the floor panting. Then I started brooding. He was patient with me. He sat on a stool and watched over me. After what seemed like a long time to me, I sighed and looked at him.

'What's going on?' I asked him weakly. 'Tell me'

He thought about it, and then he said 'A car crash was reported to the Met. Tumbled down a cliff and had a bit of a burn. Didn't mean anything to us in homicide until first responders said there were three people in the car. One was shot four times. The other's neck was broken. The driver had his throat crushed and almost torn out. We were invited in to piece together what might have happened'

'Why you?' I asked. 'You were busy with me when the call came'

'Our visit to you was not yet official; my team was free and they needed Clara's expertise. She looks at a crime scene and works out what happened. I thought that was just Sherlock Holmes until I started working with Clara. She shocks me the things she can do'.

I remembered the illuminate green eyes.

And I remembered the girl I saw at the hotel reception. I was becoming a fan of this girl!! There was this stand-out aura I saw in that brief glimpse in the hotel lobby earlier today that just shouted 'woman of substance'. Call it a psychiatric thing but I liked her. She seemed like an outright straight arrow. That quality trips me a lot.

... Ok; fine; I was identifying with the unappreciated. Tough! Sue me.

'She already linked the call to your girlfriend before we left your house yesterday. She told me that your girl was not pushed. That she was holding something back. That she may have committed a crime. She told me this just as we left your house'

'I saw you look at me'

'Exactly. I was asking Clara why she didn't want to give you protection. She said you didn't need it. That someone else your girl had refused to divulge, needed the protection from her rather. Clara was of the view if they wanted her to disappear, they wouldn't push her. They would take her to a lonely place, shoot her in the head and bury her. That was where they were going but we believe your girl reacted unexpectedly and things did not go as planned. Your girl underestimated our gullibility, or Clara's gullibility; because I believed her. She must have reckoned that the car would burn to a crisp but it didn't. We processed the crime scene. The victims...'

'My friends?'

'Just the driver was your friend Ken Stanford ...'

Even as he said it, it cut my heart. Yeah they have not been good friends. Yes they were as mean as wolves. But they were my friends. My wolves.

'... the other two were some hired guns, but they were expensive hired guns. They knew their jobs well. We knew them. Linked to about seven murders but we have not been able to prove anything. They were that good. And the three of them could not handle your girl. They were armed. She was not. How did she overpower them? How did she rip out your friend's throat? Yes. The MD told us. Your friend's throat was ripped out with fingers. Fingers! How did she do that? How did she get out of an out of control moving vehicle before it went off a cliff and was still calm with presence of mind? How ...' He stalled and pondered

I stared at him speechless.

'Clara thinks she is some kind of an elite special unit girl. You know why? Because after the car crashed, as it was still burning, she went into it and removed everything that would link her to the crime scene including Mr Stanford's phone. No fingerprints were in the car that has not been identified. There's no proof she was there. She was that cold, calm, calculating with complete presence of mind. She even remembered not to touch anything. That meant she knew ... she knew she was going to get out'

'How do you know all this? You were not there'

'Because by midnight, your friend Mike called the police station and demanded protection in exchange for information. He told us some crazy stuff that actually checked out. He told us of the plan to eliminate your girl; how they monitored her routine and noted days she went to the mall; how they tried to delay you in the office with the bogus client while they waited for her to leave for the mall; his attempt to delay you at the shopping mall while Brill and his group packed her stuff in your house; how you almost saw her being taken away by Ken's group while he talked with you; how he kept in constant discussion with Ken on the way to make her disappear and how the phone suddenly went into crackles and he never heard Ken again. There was no phone at the crime scene or within a fifteen-mile radius'

'How did he know it was my girl's fault?'

'Because she is still alive. They were supposed to take her to an unknown destination and shoot her there. Because he said that after the crackles stopped, a calm female voice called him by name and said and I quote "Ken isn't coming. But I am" and the line went dead. There was only one female in that car. There was only one female that was in the whole operation. He said he knew she was dangerous but did not expect instant justice the same day. He was beside himself in fear when he called us. Brill had called him and said someone was in his house. All his guards had been put down. Thirty minutes after that call, we got a call from Brill's girlfriend. Apparently Brill had fallen down the stairs and broken his neck, his arm and his rib. Information came to Mike. He panicked and called us. I would have dismissed it as a crank caller but Clara; she's something. She sensed something was up and she stayed late expecting the call. I don't know why but when it came, she organised protection for Mike. She reckoned that if her suspicions about your girl were true, your girl would want to tie up loose ends that might prove contrary to the story she told. She reckoned your girl was going to act fast before any witness had time to talk. She reckoned that your girl only came back to the house to make sure you were safe and then tie off loose ends. Your girl did not anticipate we would be here when she came back, and due to time constraints, she had to reveal herself and cook up a story on the spot. In as much as I thought it was a good story, but Clara picked it apart and your girl knew. So, it was important to her to tie up those loose ends before her window closed. Clara even reckoned that your girl monitored our discussion before showing herself, to make sure we were not the enemy. There is a possibility she was already here before we arrived. If you remember, we didn't even hear her come across the front lawn and the front door was open. That's saying a lot because I know Clara's instincts. I know my instincts but I know Clara's instincts. She is like a cat with her hunches and she did not detect your girl. She said she felt eyes on her when we arrived but felt it was just nosey neighbours; and when she looked around, there was nothing for her to get worried about. What if your girl meant us harm? Who is this girl?

Anyway, Clara reckoned Mike Stanford was going to be attacked same night and not after. At 1a.m., she decided she wanted to go to Mike's house. I was almost beside myself but I have come to respect deeply, Sergeant Clara's instincts so we went. Guess what, protection was down. The policemen were unconscious. We went in. We encountered a perp, dressed in all black, face covered; who knocked us about in a way that made me realize there was some lethal training there. Had no fear of the fact we had guns. Took my gun away in a move I could not understand and did something to the gun that dismembered it completely. I don't even want to think about that. That's how we got the bruises and the pain in my ribs. Clara was not fazed by the snake-like pinpoint moves of this perp. But then Clara has never been afraid of anything. Once pulled a kid out of a burning tower block and threw

herself through the window of the 8th floor hoping to get lucky. Lucky?!! Gets me sweating every time I think about it. Anyway, she gave chase but the person escaped. We saw Mike in his bathtub. He was almost drowned but not quite. Turned out he used to be in the Olympic swimming team and could hold his breath for a long time. Our presence in his house had made the perp try to make a quick getaway. We took him to the hospital. This is where it got very interesting. You see, we suspected, or Clara suspected that your girl was the mastermind behind all this, getting revenge on the people that tried to kill her but she hired someone to give herself an alibi. Mike came to an hour ego and swears your girl was the one in his house – IN PERSON'

I had heard it all. I started laughing although there was a sick feeling in my gut. But I kept laughing.

'That's absurd. I was in bed with my girl through the night. She never left my side. We were sleeping' I cried

'Maybe you were. But she wasn't'

I remembered the bandages on her arms but I pushed the thought away as fast as it had come.

'And you have concluded that without even hearing her side. Has it even occurred to you that Mike might be framing my girl? They wanted to kill her!! Your perpetrator was wearing a mask!!'

'He has already admitted to the conspiracy. He knows he's going to jail so why lie? Besides, he said he will produce infallible evidence. Also, Clara, can smell a lie a mile away. She believed him. That's enough for me'

'Maybe for you. But not for me. No one willingly comes to the police, knowing they will go to jail, unless they were coerced. I'm going to need that evidence. Otherwise I will fight this in court. And it won't be pretty'

'What other evidence would you need? Mike is alive and he will testify'

'I will need more than Mike's frivolities. I will rip him apart in court'

Alfred tossed that over in his mind.

'I can't even believe he could do this' I continued. 'He is the most gentle and kind of us all. Always peaceful and always seeing sense. Backing me up when others wanted to go crazy'

'Really? From what we have so far, he seemed to be the one coordinating the whole thing. He's the leader. The rest answer to him. And it gets bigger than you think'

I stared at him.

It suddenly just dawned on me I didn't have any friends!! These guys systematically cut me off everybody else. I don't know how they did that or why. But I ended up not having anyone at all. The thought still breaks my heart as I am talking to you right now. I was surrounded by people who did not mean me well for years without knowing it. It does a lot to your psyche. You develop trust issues. It destroys you.

Mathew, one of Alfred's team members popped his head through the door. 'We are done for now, Sir'

'I'm going back to the station' Alfred said gently to me and nodded to Mathew who withdrew.

'I'm coming with you' I said and started getting to my feet. 'It is getting quite clear to me that I will not be losing any night sleep on my friends'

'Nobody will. But she shouldn't have taken the law into her hands. Now she will be paying for it needlessly' Alfred said and led the way. I grimly followed.

XVIII

The police station was bustling. Everyone was busy. Reporters were trying to glean as much information as they could from any available cop. Phones were ringing off the hook. A lot of concerned connections of my friends wanted more information each for his or her own selfish ends. I was maligned so nobody seemed to be asking about me. I didn't care. We met Clara walking down the corridor with Owen, one of the detectives. He was holding a piece of black clothing.

'Send it to Forensics. Let me know what they find' Clara was saying.

'Will do' Owen said and headed off down the opposite corridor.

Clara had a file with her heading to the interrogation room.

'Hey; how are we doing?' Alfred asked her

'All set. She's waiting for me'

'Mr Reynolds feels we got the wrong person. He will vouch for her alibi'

Clara glanced at me. 'Okay. Then this will interest you' And she moved on

'What? What will interest me?' I asked

'This way sir' And Alfred headed for another room. I followed.

The room was a bit dark with a wide one-way mirror into the interrogation room. I could see Enigma sitting quietly, handcuffed to the table. A cop was standing by the door. I could see her but she could not see me as the mirror would only give back reflections of her. She seemed comfortable as if she were used to these kinds of scenes. Her face was relaxed and she played with her fingers like a child. My brain just could not compute all that had been said about her. It just could not.

Despite the events of the dark alley the first night but c'mon; that was self-defence and she had taken those yobs by surprise. She confessed same. This was a sweet childlike girl with the sweetest heart.

'How are you, David?'

I turned and the police chief was sitting in the corner observing my girl.

'This must be important for you to be here' I said.

He looked at me. 'It's a murder case. It's breaking news. The whole country is interested. They will need answers'

I watched as Clara stepped into the room, placed the file in front of her and sat down opposite Enigma. Enigma looked up at her with the bored expression. They stared at each other awhile.

'Do we start pitching wit against wit, or are you going to tell me the truth?' Clara asked

Enigma's expression did not change.

'Okay. Wit it is then' And Clara opened the file. 'The charge against you has changed. It is now three murders and one attempted murder'

Enigma's expression did not change

'What is she talking about?' I asked Alfred whose expression showed he did not know either as he leaned forward in interest.

'I can see you're not in the least surprised' Clara continued

'What's your proof?' Enigma quietly asked

'Ah'. Clara switched on a video feed and gestured to Enigma to watch. I saw someone walk into frame and drop a set of files on his desk. There was a distinct click in the background as if something moved. He froze and spun around.

'Why, that's Sani' I said, not recognizing my voice

'Who are you? How did you get in here?!' Sani cried

Camera field view widened to accommodate the whole room. My curiosity was triggered. This was not some off chance recording from some planted security camera. Somebody was manipulating it at the time of this incident. I was not alone in my thoughts

'Somebody was watching this play out' Alfred said in intrigue

Then she came into view, dressed in all black including gloves and a balaclava shrouded in a hood. She was leaning on the wall in the shadows. She sighed and pushed herself off the wall.

'Sorry; I didn't know there was a file on the floor' came the sonorous voice

'I recognize that figure' Alfred said. Then he looked at me. 'That's the same person we encountered in Mike's house'

Sani scrambled to a switch and the room was illuminated.

'Who are you?!' He roared

She stared at him for an unnerving moment

'I was just leaving' She said and headed for the door

'Who are you?!! What are you doing here?! How did you get in here?!!' Sani challenged desperately, moving cautiously towards the figure

She looked at him and continued towards the door.

Sani roared and rushed at her. He had always been a volatile man. The figure in black had some exquisite moves. In a split second, she had moved out of grasp, stepped away from his path and left him reeling to the wall. He spun around and glared at the figure. She was quietly observing him from another corner of the room, her head cocked to one side.

'It is you, isn't it? Does he know you're here?' Sani asked.

The figure did not reply.

'I know it is you. But the coward in you won't let you reveal your face and look me in the eye' Sani said 'Rather you'd keep sneaking about and not even making a good job of it. Good operatives will come and go without your knowing'

She kept looking at him.

'How long have you been here?' Sani asked 'What did you hear?'

'Enough' she said calmly

Sani was breathing rage. 'What are you going to do?'

She stared at him, quiet and still

'What are you going to do?!!' Sani roared

'A lot' She said quietly

Sani roared and rushed at her. The rage and venom in the rush was quite poignant to say the least.

Her hands moved in a blur and he slammed the side of his face on the wall and sprawled on the floor in a heap. She moved to a more vantage point, still looking at him. Sani regained his breath and clambered to his feet, stared at her briefly, then grabbed a stool and rushed at her again. Some lightening moves and the stool clanged away, Sani grunted and were in a heap again on the floor, wincing and breathing hard. She removed her mask and in truth, it was Enigma. She had the flat eyes and they were keenly observing Sani. She had her hair tied back in a low ponytail.

My mouth dropped open. How did she know where Sani lived? When did she go there?!

'Some moves you got there' Clara said, observing the video with actual intrigue although I noticed those illuminate green eyes were as flat as a mamba's. 'I encountered those same moves in Mike's house last night'

I looked at Enigma in the interrogation room. She had moved her eyes away from the video and back on the table, her face grim.

'I didn't know they had a camera in there as well' she muttered

'As well?' Clara countered. 'You knew about the rest?'

Enigma did not answer. She kept her gaze on the table, her face set; her eyes flat.

Even though I was looking at the feed and seeing her there, a part of me still did not want to believe it. If she had said it wasn't her, I would have believed her; even defended her. This calm quiet comment of hers threw me. I was shocked. I didn't know this girl at all. Who was she?

"Really?!! Now?!! You had lived with her for close to 6 months and you didn't know her name!! And you were surprised you didn't know who she was?!"

Don't chew me up. It all got swallowed up in pet names. I called her "Sweets" and she called me "Snacks". It got to a point, I just couldn't ask her real name anymore, you see. Felt it was ridiculous to ask.

Besides, I meant, why was she here? Why was she in my life?

Let me finish my story.

Snacks? Snacks!! This lady ate my food!!

Clara paused the video, studied Enigma briefly and said 'You didn't know. There were cameras in everyone's office, everyone's house, everyone's car. We will get to that' and she switched the video feed back on

I was just staring at them in shock. Everyone's house? Everyone's car? What was this; Big Brother?

Enigma's voice on the video feed made me turn back to the video.

'Are you gonna keep this up?' She asked

'I know who you are!' Sani snarled

'Yeah? I hear you've been asking. So, who am I?'

'You were supposed to be dead'

'But I'm not! That was the only part of his business you didn't know about and that's why I'm still alive. I read the files. I listened to your meetings. I put two and two together. What do you think is going through my mind now?'

'You're not going to kill me. You will never get away with it. And you will lose him forever'

'If I wanted you dead, you'll be dead'

'Wrong. You want us dead. But you cannot. Because it has not been sanctioned' Sani straightened up, his face intent. 'We've been asking for sure. You're not supposed to be here. And yet here you are. You think you are special because of what he did for you? You are nothing! He does that every day for everybody! He doesn't even remember he did it for you!'

She smiled through clenched teeth 'And that Mr Rasheed is what makes him special. So I can't in all conscience let anything happen to him. You want him dead. Someone who had been your friend and loved you all these years'.

'My friend?' Sani spat on the floor. 'I am going to hurt him. He will beg for death before it comes'.

Enigma stared at him as she let that sink in.

'Mr Rasheed; killing him will make me upset; and you really do not want to see me upset'. Her eyes were glazed as she quietly picked those words.

'We will starve him; we will stick needles in him and we will send him to Shamarin. What are you going to do?' Sani asked

She gave him the deadpan stare, but her chest was heaving. She was getting angry. Sani did not notice. Without another word, she headed for the door.

'You are not supposed to be here. That means all you know has not gone anywhere because you are unaccounted for by your agency' Sani said. She stopped and looked at him. 'You know our plans. You know what we intend for you. But you don't care about yourself, I know. But then I ask: What becomes of Mr Reynolds if you're out of the picture today, I wonder' and with that, Sani opened one of his drawers and swiped a pistol and pointed it at her.

My hands went to my mouth in utter shock. Pistol!! How did he get that? They are not even legal. My own friend! I did not recognize the Sani on the video feed.

She on the other hand gave him the bored look. He squeezed the trigger and there was a distinct click. I flinched in shock.

He did it! He actually squeezed the trigger to kill in cold blood!

She did not move. He squeezed it a couple more times growling in frustration. She pulled out a clip from her pocket and showed it to him.

Sani looked at his pistol in rage

'You've been here awhile' he said. 'Long before the meeting started'

'Like I said, I heard enough' she said

He flung the pistol at her. She moved her head a fraction and the pistol went by. Sani roared, grabbed a nearby bottle and launched himself at her. I was shocked at the intensity. He sure didn't mean her well.

I never knew she could move so fast. Within seconds it was over. She had side stepped him, knocked the bottle away, lashed a few punches to his face and trunk, then clipped his weight-bearing foot. Grunting all the way, Sani fell awkwardly, hit his head on a mahogany side stool on his way down and became still.

'I'm not getting out of the picture yet. I will tell him the truth about his friends and let the cards cascade however they may' she said. 'It ends today' and she turned to leave. Then she paused and looked at Sani. 'Mr Rasheed? Mr Rasheed?' Then she ran to him and looked. Then she bit her lip in utter despair, snapped her fingers in frustration and stared. It was obvious this was not part of the plan. 'Damn it damn it damn it' She whispered fiercely. Then she started looking around.

'That was the day Sani died?' I asked Alfred morosely. He nodded. 'She was with me at home all night'

Alfred gave me the look.

I turned back to the video feed, my face a picture of flabbergast. She had grabbed the bottle of alcohol, forced Sani's mouth open, tipped his chin up, poured half the contents in, massaged his throat and did some tandem compressions on his chest and abdomen.

'That trick is amazing. You gotta teach me sometime' Clara said

Some of the alcohol spilled all over, but three-quatres of the content went into his stomach. She poured the rest of the contents on his shirt and around his shoes, smearing a puddle under his foot. She put the bottle in his right hand and smashed it on the ground beside the body. Then she arranged the room as best she could, put the clip back into the pistol, put it back into the drawer, put her mask back on and was out of the room.

Everyone on my side of the room had the same face you have right now including me.

"My goodness"

"Her proficiency... her fast thinking... the ability to find a detailed solution at the spur of the moment. Yes. Apparently, most nights when I slept, she wasn't. The thought still overwhelms me. How efficient she was. Forensics went through that room and couldn't pick her out. Autopsy looked at the body and did not see any foul play. How did she do that? How could she achieve that? How ...."

"Anyway, I noticed no one on my side of the room was talking.

119

They were just looking at each other. Clara turned off the feed and stared at Enigma. Enigma did not return the stare. She kept her gaze on her fingers"

'I'm told there are a lot more where that came from, including the encounter with Brill and what actually happened in the car with Ken. I'm told those are very interesting. IT department is still going through the lot'

Enigma still did not look up.

'This is what we have so far. It is part of a syndicate with a plan to start a new world order. They are operating from Asia, but their main focus is the destabilization of Europe. Mr Staples is the leader of this cell in London. He doesn't know how many cells there are. But he knows every cell reports to a particular engine elsewhere. They know who you are. You know who they are. Mr Reynolds was just caught in the middle because he became your friend. They discovered you were some kind of an elite special forces Soldier who was investigating Mr Reynold's charities and shipping line'

My heart did a summersault

'My ... Wha ... She was investigating my business? Why was she investigating my business?' I asked, looking at Alfred who kept silent, still observing

'They found out you were onto them and they didn't want to be exposed. Orders came for you to be discreetly eliminated without spooking Mr Reynolds. So they tried a charade. They tried to destroy the relationship so you would leave Mr Reynolds. Then they will eliminate you. They didn't expect Mr Reynolds to become deeply emotionally involved with you.'

Enigma's face twitched and she clenched and unclenched her fists.

'Who would?' Clara continued 'Everyone knew him as a player. They didn't expect his stubborn resolve to make the relationship work no matter what was thrown at him.'

Enigma blinked and looked away.

Clara continued 'Then the destabilizing move: They didn't anticipate you will confront Sani and try to push him to make a mistake by telling him you will tell Mr Reynolds the truth about his friends and destroy all their plans. You thought Sani was the leader. You were expecting Mr Reynolds would get the police involved. I presume your plan was, while the police did their job, you would protect Mr Reynolds from any untoward harm. You did not anticipate Sani would die that night. But things went wrong and he did. You went into a panic because that destroyed your whole plan and you couldn't make the big reveal to Mr Reynolds anymore because no one will believe you with murder hanging over your head. You will be taken away and Mr Reynolds will be left unprotected. The thought of that terrified you. So you covered it up by making it look like an unintentional accident and continued with the charade. But Mike knew it was not an accident because it was he who had a video feed installed in every one's office, cars and home without their knowing or consent. Made it easier for him to coordinate things. He even hired the car that was used for your abduction and planted the camera in it. He revealed his knowledge of Sani's death to the rest without telling them how he knew because that would bring suspicion and destroy everything. But because they know he always had a way of getting information, they believed him without questions. They decided to move their plans forward due to pressure from elsewhere. Mike has refused to open up on who "elsewhere" is. The plan was still to take you out and make it look like you went away because you could not stand the pain David was going through. I bought that story myself. It was important to them to keep their David angle intact because it was so good it was unreal. And since you were unaccounted for by your agency, it seemed fool proof. They made their plan, but things went wrong because as you said, they didn't know how nasty you can get when you are upset. Poor souls. First time I met you, I knew I wouldn't want to see you upset. But they didn't because Mike could not tell them the truth of what he saw in the video feed, so they underestimated you. When Mr Brill popped up dead, Mike knew the game was up. The Syndicate was displeased they had failed and he was instructed to self-terminate to prevent any link to the syndicate. Being the coward he is, he went into a panic and spilled the beans to us for protection. Did I miss anything?'

Enigma was silent.

'Here's my question: What did he mean by you were supposed to be dead?'

Everyone on my side of the room leaned forward.

Enigma did not look up.

'See, I know all these were in self-defence. The reason I know is because you didn't kill the policemen at Mr Staples'. All the law enforcement personnel you encountered, you only knocked out. But you wiped out the bodyguards at Mr Brill's. So in truth, you are actually a good guy. I just want to know the truth. How you got involved. Why you got involved. Which Agency you are working with. Who sent you. I'm actually on your side' Clara said.

Enigma smiled and she was stunning when she smiled.

"Really? Are you still saying that?"

'You are not on my side' Enigma said. Then she looked at Clara. 'No one is on my side. If David were here, he wouldn't be on my side. And this was all for him. I'm alone here. And I know it. I'm used to it. So please don't insult me with the empathy card'

'You knew Mr Reynolds wouldn't be on your side. So why do it?' Clara asked

Enigma stared at Clara a bit 'He deserves it'

'What do you mean?'

'There are men. And there is David Reynolds. He is a rare specimen. He didn't deserve what they were planning'

'So you are willing to ruin your life because of him?'

Enigma smiled and looked away.

'Who sent you to protect him?' Clara asked

'No one. I'm alone here'

Clara cocked her head to one side as she observed Enigma. 'Your accent; you are American. You've been switching from British to American accents at will since we met. Maybe an unintentional slip. But I picked it.

'What's your point?'

'Something is not sitting right with me. You don't just wake up one morning, travel a hundred and fifty thousand miles across the world to destroy your life over a man. Not someone as intelligent as you. Mr Reynolds is not the most desirable man in the world. There are hundreds better than him. He is not even in the first two thousand....'

'Alright; steady on' I muttered to myself

' ... And a woman that looks like you, with all your qualities; that can get any man she damn well pleases, decides he is the one that is worth it all? That makes you a fool! And you don't look a fool to me. And if something doesn't sit right with me, it usually isn't the truth. So tell me the truth. I want to know what it is that made you throw yourself into the deep end and flush your life down a toilet for a man you met in a damn Soho nightclub party for the first time in your life'

'It's not the first time' Enigma muttered.

Clara stared at her

I was confused. I exchanged glances with everyone in my side of the room and shrugged my ignorance.

'He visited me in the hospital once. I remember the perfume. I remember the voice. He wouldn't know. I was wrapped in bandages and feeding through a tube. He thought I was in a coma. But

I heard every sweet and kind word he said. I felt the care in his voice. He was pleased I was alive. I don't understand how a man could be like that. To someone you don't know'

'What are you talking about?' Clara asked

Enigma looked at her 'The truth. Switch off the recording and I will give you details'

'Why?'

'Privileged information. Off records'

'I'll be the judge of that' Clara said and Enigma clamped shut.

They stared at each other for a long time. I almost screamed 'shut the damn records off!!'

As if Clara heard me, she suddenly sighed and switched the recording off.

'Go on' she said

Enigma looked at the recording to be sure the red light was off.

'If what I am about to say leaves this room, I will deny it. And I will be upset'

'The recording is not on' Clara said mildly. Then encouraged her with her eyes.

'He saved my life' Enigma said.

'How do you mean?' Clara asked

'I was caught behind enemy lines in Shamarin, Syria. Everyone denied my presence there. Expected because of the kind of job I was doing' Enigma started

'What kind of job was that? Recon?' Clara asked

'Hardly important. The information I had obtained had already been used. There was no way of getting me out. The risks outweighed the gains. I was abandoned to die; my file closed. The terrorist cell that had me decided to keep me alive a while longer for their pleasure. I was going to die – but slowly. I was going to pray for death and I was going to be stretched before that prayer was answered. They were good at it. Two weeks into my keep, a renegade detachment of mercenaries broke through enemy lines and found me and brought me home. They were sponsored by an establishment who happened to come across my story'

'David Reynolds' Clara said

'He'd never met me. He didn't know me. He just heard about me. Hired investigators to locate me. Sponsored a recruitment of mercenaries willing to go behind enemy lines with a 13% chance of success. Paid my hospital bills and rehabilitation. Cost him 8 million pounds to run that programme'. Tears welled in her eyes. 'He didn't know me. He had never met me. I was not some friend. I wasn't even an acquaintance. I was expendable. Trash. Forgotten. Not to him. I was worth eight million to him. Someone he'd never met. Someone he stood to gain nothing from'.

I noticed the policemen on my side looking at me. There was deep respect in their eyes. I couldn't meet their gaze. I looked down demurely.

She sighed and continued 'I was not supposed to know who he was. Those were his instructions. But I got to know when we found out that 9 of his charity establishments were being used to launder money for terrorist cells...'

I froze and looked up, my mouth agape. As she talked, I kept gasping in shock.

'... and he didn't know about it. His ships were being used to move weapons. His trusted friends were the contacts for these cells. They befriended him solely for this purpose. They wanted to use him. Gave him connections that bolstered his earnings and made him trust them. Blocked off everyone else and surrounded him with their own people. He didn't know. The buck was supposed to stop with him. If things went south, he was going to take the brunt of it all; get incarcerated or even ...' she choked '... die.

Counter terrorism was going to shut him down and destroy him. I lobbied hard. There was no way someone like that could be a terrorist. No way!'

'How do you know?'

'No way!'

'I asked, how do you know?'

Enigma stared at her 'A hunch'.

They stared at each other. I would have given a lot to know what each one was thinking.

Clara swallowed 'So what happened?'

'I volunteered to get evidence. CT turned me down. Felt I might spook him and jeopardize all the work they had put in. They didn't even consider his friends. Like I said, the buck stopped with him. I had two weeks on my sabbatical, so I decided to come here and observe him. I didn't believe my luck when he made contact. Spent two weeks with him, searched his house, searched his office, went through his contacts, monitored his harbour, ships and staff, and tailed him through his liaisons. There was no proof of any of these transactions except that it was happening with his ships'

'How did you pick up on his friends?'

'I saw the camera in his house and noticed it was a remote feed. Someone was watching him. I got my contact to find out who. Turned out it was Mike Staples and he always had meetings with the others – without Mr Reynolds; at odd hours of the morning on particular days. I let the camera be not to spook them but I decided to start attending those meetings uninvited and latent. Found out a lot of things. Also found out they have been asking about me as well and did not like the information they were getting. I didn't know the camera had a microphone as well because the day I told Mr Reynolds I was a soldier was the day they started asking about me and discovered I was the soldier left behind in

Syria. That's when I realised Staples had access to military grade equipment. There was a sponsor elsewhere and my presence in town and in David's life was making them very uncomfortable. Mr Sani was correct. I was supposed to be dead. I was the only operation after they became his friends that Mr Reynolds had done without telling anyone. He had tried four times before me for other soldiers and his money had been wasted and the soldiers had been killed. I found out his friends were the ones sabotaging the operations. He confided in them. This time around because of the cell keeping me was an exceptionally ruthless one with genocidal reputation, his friends felt they didn't need to bother. I was a lost cause. Mr Reynolds decided to go ahead with it despite. It makes him feel good to be kind to someone; especially someone who can't say 'thank you'. And he's tenacious with it. That's why I survived. I read the files. Three groups of mercenaries had turned him down after taking his money. Yet he persisted. The renegade group that agreed charged double the price he offered. He paid. He didn't know me. I still can't understand it. He stood to gain nothing from me' She sniffed and blinked back tears. 'Who can be that kind?!'

Clara looked down and swallowed

'I listened to the meetings his friends had when they obtained the information he was the sponsor of the operation' Enigma continued 'Elsewhere was angry with them so they were seething against him. I felt it in the room. My survival was something Elsewhere did not like and they blamed Mr Reynolds for it. Then to make matters worse, I had made Mr Reynolds cancel a travel plan to Kuwait they had arranged with him long before I came in. A travel he was not supposed to come back from. I heard. That set them back so much. Elsewhere was livid'.

I stared in horror.

'They were planning some terrible things for him' Enigma said

'Someone as famous as Mr Reynolds will be missed; surely' Clara countered

'They had plans' Enigma quietly said. 'They were enthusiastic about it. They were certain it would worked'. She took a deep breath and with deep intent said 'I just couldn't let that happen. I can't. I won't'

Clara stared at her a bit, lost in thought. Then she cleared her throat 'So you stayed and became AWOL, sacrificing everything'

'If you were in my shoes, what would you do?'

'I won't be going to jail for murder' Clara said, a crease on her forehead

Enigma smiled 'Yes you will'

'No. I will not' Clara said emphatically

'You're not getting the point, detective. I died in Syria. My life belongs to him' She looked away at the far wall 'Mr Sani died that night because I was distracted. The thought of David hurting while thinking he was losing friends ate me up; made me careless. I stepped on a file on the floor. That was rooky mistake. It wasn't supposed to happen. That night wasn't supposed to end that way'. She sighed and looked down as if she were ashamed.

Clara stared at her for a while; then sighed, looked down and muttered 'So you fell in love with him'

Enigma looked up and stared at her. Clara looked up to meet the gaze

'Wouldn't you?' Enigma asked

'Lady, we don't think alike' Clara said 'A lot I would have done differently'

Enigma grunted. 'Funny. I didn't know that'

They both observed each other.

There was a knock on the door and Mason, one of the unit detectives popped in. 'We just got a call from the hospital. Mike Staples just died'

Clara stared at him.

In my room, Alfred jumped to his feet and headed for the door at once. 'Stay here, Sir. Someone will take you home' and he was out.

'Why? He was stable when we left him. The doctor said he was going to be alright' Clara was saying

'He may have developed a complication. The doctor said his heart stopped' Mason said. 'They couldn't save him'

Clara and Enigma looked at each other and did that communication thing with their eyes.

'I'm heading over there. Where is the lieutenant?' Mason said.

'"Elsewhere"?' Enigma said and Clara's eyes narrowed.

'Secure the scene, Mason. Let no one in or out. If they have CCTV, I want to see it' Clara said and jumped to her feet as Mason left. She turned to the uniformed policeman 'Take her back to her cell' and headed for the door.

'Detective' Enigma whispered.

Clara turned. They observed each other. Enigma sighed.

'I won't be able to do anything from the cell' Enigma said. 'He's so innocent, he's naked'

Clara stared at her for a brief while 'He's stupid'

Enigma swallowed. 'And that too'

Clara sighed and left the room.

I watched as they took Enigma away, my whole mind a buzz. I didn't know what to make of this. I still don't. I went home that night, my mind a daze. I was incommunicado for a week, just tossing and turning in bed, unable to do anything reasonable. I was lonely. I was miserable. It became all too clear to me without a doubt that I wasn't the lovable all-powerful dude I thought I was. I was just a pawn in a sick game; a mule for terrorists. Here I was thinking my life was boring, not knowing I was in the middle of espionage that could have drastically changed the world, not to talk of the possibility of death.

Me!

Killed!

Dead.

I felt cold. I felt sick. I felt lethargic. Aimless. Like a zombie.

I didn't feel like talking to anyone. I didn't even contact Florence and all her attempts to contact me were ignored. I spent most days staring into space and brooding. Some days I forgot to bathe or wash my mouth or even eat. I grew a beard Robinson Crusoe would have envied. My house became a bit too unkempt because I didn't care. My cleaner's contract had been terminated since I started with Enigma on her say so. I missed Enigma. I missed her. So much. So much.

I remembered her warning: 'If I stay, you can't get me out of your system'.

My goodness. Everything she had said was so correct. She never trifled with words.

Everything had a deep meaning and full of impact.

I shuddered at the realisation that I was in for a long period of pain and misery because boy; I missed her!!!

I was this close ... this close ... this close to ending it all. There was an emptiness that overwhelmed me. My heart was wrenched out by her absence. How could a woman do that to a man? How? The thought of how I felt those times sends chills through me. I will not want to feel that ever again. Come to think of it, I don't know how I survived those days. Probably because I didn't want those bastards to think they won. Maybe that's what it is. I don't know.

I thought I had friends. I had no friends. And oh, how I missed Enigma. The house felt hollow and empty without her. A part of me died when she was taken away. I know I will never recover that part of me again. It's gone. I didn't want to believe everything I heard there. And yet it was true! I have been living with a cold-blooded killer and I didn't know it.

"To be fair to her, she told you the truth. She's a soldier. She went where others couldn't. That explained how dangerous and lethal she was. Your friends pushed her. They yanked her tiger's tail, so to speak. What were you expecting?"

"I guess something had to give. She was too perfect, wasn't she? Besides, I was looking for an excuse to douse this volcano of pain that was twirling inside me running me crazy. How could a woman have such an effect on someone? It was uncanny. It was unnatural. Everything in the house reminded me of her. I couldn't even go to the bathroom without wondering how she sat when she was in the bathroom. I only watched movies she liked. I only wore clothes she liked. I slept on the side of the bed she used to lie on. Arranged things the way she wanted them arranged. Sang songs she used to hum to herself when she was in the kitchen. I also went to -"

I had to cut him short!

"You didn't go to visit her?"

"And say what? I couldn't bring myself to. Couldn't face her. Didn't know what I would say. Our relationship was a lie? She was investigating me when I thought she cared about me? And yet she did everything for me. She sacrificed everything for me. What if she had found something? Something incriminating? Then what? Would she have taken me out? Killed me? What decision would she have made? I didn't know if I wanted to know the answers to those questions. I didn't know how to process the whole situation. My mind was a haze. My heart was broken. I couldn't handle human associations anymore. I went into a shell and stayed there.

Then someday, auspiciously, Pauline came calling. I don't know why I did; but I let her in. lucky I did. Because I know I was definitely at the brink...

XIX

Pauline was the first I met. Through Sani it was. She was lovely, sweet and pure. She also knew how to meet you at your time of need. She just understood, you know. She came to check on me after hearing all about what happened. This was quite surprising considering all that transpired. I wasn't sure what she really wanted. Was I now forgiven? Are we about to start a relationship again? I wanted to know. So I asked her. I know that sounds callous, but I wanted to be sure. I wasn't ready for anything.

'I'll be stupid to date you, David' she said. 'As a matter of fact, I'm insulted you would even think that. You're not God's gift to women, you know'

And I had to spend the day apologising. I was just weary. She forgave me and being her usual sweet self, still made herself available to me, cooking and cleaning and sitting with me through the day sometimes. God! I needed that. She was a listening ear to my babbles through some days.

And some nights.

She came daily. I can say she was a reason I never ran crazy. Kept me sane. At some point, I looked forward to her coming like a dope addict would look forward to a fix. She never disappointed.

Gradually warmth started getting into my heart. I started to laugh again. My first chuckle to a joke she made was 6 months to the day after Enigma's arrest. She celebrated it by dancing a Kozachok. We started to share jokes and play. Gradually I started going out to dinner once again, but it was baby steps. As I enjoyed it more, I became more and more grateful to Pauline than I have ever been. I gradually started putting ideas on paper once more and started getting back to work. As I felt more life come back into me, the more confident I became to create more ideas and prepare to face the world again. Next thing I did was to remove everything in my house that reminded me of Enigma. I removed the plates and pots she used to use for our dinners and gave them to charity. I burned the bedsheets and cushions in my house and replaced them with new ones. I even changed the arrangement of stuff in my kitchen and scattered the shoes in my wardrobe – just anything to make me forget the angelic damsel.

"Did it work?" I asked

"Well, I felt liberated enough to start a good partnership with Pauline. I had pulled the plug on all indicted charities, reviewed the rest and revamped my shipping staff. My partnership with Pauline was going to conglomerate all my international endeavours. Since people were finding it hard to trust me, Pauline was going to front it. We garnered support and strategized. She made it work. The day the green light was given, I was so happy, we went to celebrate. One thing led to another and I guess you can say we entered the twilight zone with a lot of fireworks.

Next morning, we woke in each other's arms but the atmosphere was a bit subdued. We both knew why. We lay quiet for a while.

'What is this, David?'

I wasn't going to lie to Pauline. 'I don't know'

She was silent for a while. 'Are you going to break my heart again?'

'It was not my intention the first time. It just happened'

'So anytime someone you feel is better than me comes up, you would just pack up and run'

'No! Please don't say that'

'That's what you're saying'

I was silent and brooding. She disentangled from me and picked up a dressing gown. Then she stared at me.

'Maybe we should keep this professional from now on'

Call me soppy or stupid but I was scared of being on my own. I was scared of the pits my mind could go to. My heart desperately needed someone to cling on to; someone that would be a reason to wake up every morning. Pauline was it for me at that moment. I wanted her in my life. She was so comforting. Call me selfish.

'What if I don't want it to be just professional?' I whined

'Then you better make up your mind. Because I'm not going to be your rebound girl. I can't go through the pain I went through the last time. I won't'

There was a knock on the door. She headed down the stairs. I climbed into a dressing gown and followed her. She got to the door and opened it.

'Hello?' She said

'Hi' the husky voice replied. 'Is Mr Reynolds around?'

I hurried out. 'Detectives'

Pauline went and sat on a sofa. The green eyes trailed her.

'Can we speak to you in private please' Alfred asked

'Oh no; Please come in. Anything you want to tell me, say it in front of Pauline' I said in all bravado.

'Ok' Alfred reluctantly said. 'Has Jane Doe contacted you?'

I frowned. 'You still don't know her name?'

'Do you?' Clara asked

Alfred glared at her as he spoke 'Her files are classified. We don't have all the permits yet. Still working on it'

'It's been a year' I said

'A lot of permits to get' Alfred said

'So why should she contact me?' I asked

'Because she escaped' Clara said. Pauline must have reacted because the illuminate green eyes looked in her direction. I turned towards Pauline. She had sat up, her face looking worried.

'What do you mean, she escaped?' I asked

'How?' Pauline cried

'She picked the lock. With a toothpick. And some strands of her hair' Clara said.

'How?' I cried.

Alfred subdued a smile and shook his head in obvious admiration but caught our eyes and jerked back to seriousness.

'Despite the fact that some people may be impressed with her …' Clara said staring at Alfred, 'but if she does contact you, you give us a call'. Then she gave Pauline a glance before flooding me with her stare and to my chagrin, I noticed her green eyes were practically glowing. A sign she was angry. 'I don't have to tell you how dangerous she is'

'She won't hurt me' I said

Clara looked at Pauline 'I know', then she looked into my eyes

'I will call, Detective' I said demurely.

And she promptly turned and walked out of the house. Alfred gave me a kinder look and followed her.

'We'll keep in touch, sir' he had said. Then he caught up with her as they walked to the car.

I stared after them wondering "what now?"

'Now I know why he never bothered to visit her once. He already had another one in his nest' I heard her say to Alfred

'It is not in our place to judge' Alfred said gently and got into the car

Clara got into the car and looked at me again. Her eyes showed her disappointment. I didn't meet her stare. She sighed and turned back to Alfred. 'Let's go find this visitor that came to see her yesterday'

The car drove off. I watched it go and sighed looking around at the houses in my quiet residence.

'That detective didn't seem to approve of me' Pauline said coming behind me

'Yes. I noticed, too. But it's her problem, not yours' I said. 'She's not my mother'

She hugged me from the back.

'I was the first; and I used to be the only' she said

I sighed 'A lot of things I will be making up for'

'Definitely' she said. Then we faced each other 'To my shame, I have a very forgiving heart'

We stared at each other

'I will make it up to you. Even if it takes my lifetime' I said

'Don't make promises you cannot keep' she said

I smiled reassuringly. 'C'mon. Let's talk upstairs' and I began to close the door. Then I felt it. There was this uncanny feeling like I was being watched. I felt this sensation down my spine. It was really odd. I paused and looked outside again. The road was quiet. The street was calm. There was just the faint drone of traffic in the distance. I sighed and closed the door.

That's where the next chapter of my life started...

Epilogue:

The waiter came over. "We are closing sir; ma'am"

"Really? So soon?" I asked

"It's 2 a.m. ma'am. We've been waiting for you. So sorry"

"That late?" David said "I have to go to bed. Let's continue tomorrow, okay"

"Aw. I was looking forward to the next chapter of your life"

David smiled. "It's a bit of a spiral. I will tell you tomorrow. I'll come to your room"

I smiled. "okay".

"Thanks for listening. It was actually therapeutic. I guess I should be paying for it sometime" He smiled

I smiled back "Good night"

He finished his drink and walked off. I gathered myself together, my mind drifting through the story I just heard. What an adventure. I still had some questions though, about some parts of the story but I guess I would have to wait for the next morning.

I still didn't get myself a good man today. Great. I headed for my room to have a warm massaging bath. Hopefully; just hopefully, I may get some sleep....

The END....

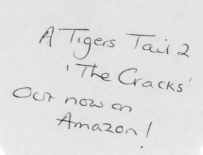

A Tigers Tail 2
'The Cracks'
Out now on
Amazon!

Printed in Poland
by Amazon Fulfillment
Poland Sp. z o.o., Wrocław

61598033R00082